The Whisperer

The Curious Janie Query Mysteries

ADDA LEAH DAVIS

Abbott Press books may be ordered through booksellers or by contacting:

Abbott Press
1663 Liberty Drive
Bloomington, IN 47403
www.abbottpress.com
Phone: 1-866-697-5310

ISBN: 978-1-4582-1721-9 (sc)
ISBN: 978-1-4582-1722-6 (e)

Library of Congress Control Number: 2014913392

Printed in the United States of America.

Abbott Press rev. date: 08/26/2014

INTRODUCTION

This, the first book in The Curious Janie Query Mystery Series, is titled "The Whisperer" because a rough, rasping whisper is the clue that helps Curious Janie Query and her friend, Prudence Leery solve the problem of how a drug ring is operating in their town.

The intent of this series is to have a new book out involving Curious Janie Query once each year. The second book "The Opening Door" is already being written.

The purpose for this series is the hope that young readers will find a new character to intrigue them and also give them the desire to read. Young people loved the Nancy Drew and the Hardy Boys mysteries and avidly read both series.

Having raised five children and taught many, many more I would hate to see a time when young people have forgotten the joy of reading. I fear that today's youth are having their imaginations dulled by the "tell-all" formats of graphic novels and some of the movies seen today.

I learned, as a child, that the building and seeing something come alive, in a new project, always sprang from a fertile imagination. If we, as children, imagined a swimming hole we set to work to build it. The building and imagining the fun we would have gave the project impetus and gave us so much pleasure that it sometimes out-weighed the finished product.

I hope young people read this series and turn their imaginations loose to take part in Curious Janie Query's adventures.

HAPPY READING!

Imagination

Give me an eye for imagination
And a quick wit to grasp the plot
And see the what if's and the wherefores
That from dreamless eyes is oft forgot.

Give me an ear to hear the wonders
That a thoughtless tongue will oft disclose
In whispered words and subtle nuances
That a staid and dreamless wit will never know.

The secret of genius is to carry the spirit of the child into old age, which means never losing your enthusiasm.

—Victor Hugo

CHAPTER 1

"Shh!" whispered Curious Janie Query as she stepped behind a huge oak tree, drawing her friend Prudence Leery with her. Somewhere to their right they heard the sounds of leaves rustling, muffled talk, and labored grunts.

This gnarled oak tree, their hiding place, had stood guard in the Garden of Eternal Peace for hundreds of years. The initials J Q for John Query, Janie's grandfather, were etched high in its bark. He was a small boy when he carved them. The tree had grown and with each passing year the initials were higher on the tree trunk. Her father had often lifted Janie up to view her grandfather's handiwork.

Prudence, who was known by everyone as Pru, was Janie's best friend and constant companion. Now she huddled closer to Janie and whispered, "What is it?"

For answer Janie reached out and luckily found Pru's face, hoping to cover her mouth, and whispered "Shh" again. They didn't dare use their flashlight even though it was nearly nine o'clock. With no moon the area was so dark that they could only dimly make out a form, but could not really see each other. Janie could see the tombstones, but now they looked like threatening ghostly silhouettes standing guard.

Janie took her hand from Pru's face, but suddenly covered it again and pulled Pru tighter against her as she shrank into the tree's rough bark.

A thud was heard as if something had fallen, followed by a minced "Drat" and the sounds were not that far away. As they shrank into the tree afraid to breathe, slow muted footsteps moved step by step, closer and closer, directly toward their hiding place.

"I'd like to know what's in this thing, wouldn't you," said a voice so close that Janie drew in a quick breath and held it. Her heart was pounding so loudly that she just knew it could be heard. She sucked in air as she felt Pru go limp and start sliding toward the ground. It was then she heard a hoarse guttural whisper.

"You don't get paid to be nosey," or that's what it sounded like to Janie. The voice was so rough and hoarse and she was holding Pru so tightly against her that she wasn't sure if she'd heard correctly.

The darkness and being dressed in indigo denim jeans and jacket were a bonus to their secrecy, as was the breadth of the tree trunk behind which they were hiding. Janie didn't think they could be seen, but unexpectedly a sliver of the moon sailed from behind a cloud, casting a dim silvery light over the scene.

Janie stood almost petrified with fear. Her arms ached with trying to hold Pru upright, but she had to keep Pru from falling. Any noise would reveal their hiding place. When the moonlight spread, Janie tried to shrink further into the tree and pulled Pru against her more tightly.

Afraid to get a deep breath, Janie stood rooted to the spot. Fear wasn't the only problem though. Breathing had become very difficult with her effort to keep Pru on her feet. Making her effort worse was Pru's elbow, which had somehow gotten against Janie's windpipe, making her feel faint. She moved her head slightly and drew in a big gulp of air just as the footsteps halted. Only the tree separated the two girls from the voices.

Janie started shaking as panic skittered through her, making her scalp tingle. She gritted her teeth, determined to withstand whatever would happen next. *Pru and I will never leave the Garden of Eternal Peace,* she thought and cringed inside.

She felt a nervous impulse to chuckle. Peace was certainly not what she was experiencing right now, for tears were slowing seeping from her eyes.

Peeping around the edge of the tree, Janic saw a tall man with a slouch hat of some dark material, drawn low over his forehead. He was breathing heavily. He stood silently turned away from their hiding place for a few seconds then groaned painfully and bending down he picked up his load. Again, he started walking slowly and heavily with each step a labored, bent-forward thrust.

That must be really heavy, thought Janie, as she listened to his labored gasps for air and watched him straining with every step. As he moved on past the tree, Janie realized that he was only carrying one end of a long box or crate. His partner on the other end of the load was hidden behind a large tombstone, but he would soon come into view.

Janie didn't get to see him though. The night was suddenly dark again as a cloud hid the moon once more.

"We'll have to lug this crate back the same way, but I'd rather do this than be down there, wouldn't you?" asked the tall man and Janie waited for the other man to answer.

When he did, his voice was the same guttural rough whisper she'd heard before. The sound came out as whispered spurts or rough whistled rasps.

"You do what you're told. It's a lot safer," or again that's what Janie thought he said. She was so scared, and as before, his spastic rough whisper was hard to understand.

Janie was becoming numb in her cramped, stilted position, and felt she might faint if she didn't soon get relief, but the footsteps finally faded away. The tall man's voice became fainter and fainter as it moved toward the main entrance of the cemetery and then was heard no more.

Janie stood still, holding Pru close to her, but when the moon slid from behind a cloud again, she released her. She fell to the ground ker-plunk.

"Ouch! Why did you knock me down?" demanded Pru as she jerked awake.

"I didn't knock you down. You fainted and I've had

to hide and hold you on your feet the whole time. You're no help at all. You didn't get to see a thing," scolded Janie.

Pru lay on the ground for a moment with a strange puzzled look on her face. Suddenly she sat up and Janie reached for her hand to help her to her feet.

"Are they gone?"

"Of course they're gone. I wouldn't have let you fall if they were still here."

Janie had forgotten to whisper, but now she lowered her voice. Suddenly it was dark again. "Let's go. We can't see a thing tonight anyway."

"Wait, my legs won't work. They're asleep." Pru whispered.

They stood waiting until Pru was recovered enough to walk. The moon slid into view again and Janie looked up at the sky. "I hope it doesn't rain. We need to come back when it's daylight and see where those two men came from. If it rains it will wash out their footprints."

"What if they are still here? They could be hiding so they can catch us," whimpered Pru softly as they were again plunged into darkness.

"Pru, it's too dark for them to see us. They wouldn't have to hide. They can't see us and we can't see them. Come on. They're gone. I guess I'll have to start believing some of Kyle Jester's wild tales."

"Turn on your flashlight, Janie. I can't see my hand in front of me. We'll fall into one of these tombstones and knock our brains out trying to walk in the dark," cautioned Pru.

"If we do, we won't have to be carried too far to be

buried. After all, this is the Garden of Eternal Peace," said Janie, chuckling as the beam from her light penetrated the smothering darkness.

Pru was eleven to Janie's twelve years, but heavier built and taller than Janie. Prudence had never been as daring as Janie, though.

"Why do we need to come back and see anything? Those men aren't bothering us. I don't like the dark especially in a cemetery. Why do you always want to check out everything you hear about, Janie?"

Just then the moon made another appearance to reveal the owlish stare of Curious Janie Query. Her glasses had slipped down and her chestnut brown pigtails hung to her waist in front of her, making her look young and shy. This was especially true when her pixie face dimpled into a broad grin at the least provocation. No one, however, had ever described Janie as shy. Janie was always called "strange, nosey, inquisitive, curious, or a busybody by those who knew her. Another characteristic that really created the name of Curious was the snow white streak through her hair that ran at an angle from above her right eye toward her right ear but stopped abruptly about half-way there.

"Isn't that a curious sight? I've never seen a child with such a mark as that. It's like the hair comes in white and grows so long and then turns brown." This comment no longer bothered Janie since she had heard it so often, nor did the term curious being tacked to her name.

"We don't need the light now so let's run. Once we're out in the road we can make our way home even if the moon is gone," said Janie, switching off the flashlight.

"If our parents knew we were out here, we'd be grounded for two weeks. I want to go to the carnival next Saturday," said Pru and they both knew that she certainly wouldn't get to go if she couldn't sneak into her room without waking her parents.

"Stop worrying Pru. You always think the worst about everything. Why would our parents check our rooms? They wouldn't dream of us being brave enough to go out at night. Anyway, my parents never come into my room after I go to bed, does yours?" asked Janie as they cleared the cemetery gate and stepped onto the road.

Pru grabbed Janie's sleeve. "A car is coming. What are we going to do?"

Janie didn't answer. Instead she shoved Pru across the road and down over the side into the woods. She slid down beside Pru and they lay flat on their stomachs until the car had passed.

"Okay, let's go," said Janie as she grabbed Pru's hand and pulled her to her knees. Pru grunted as she crawled back to the roadway and stood up.

"Did you get hurt?" asked Janie, flashing her light into Pru's face.

"Get that light out of my face. I can't see a thing, and no, I didn't get hurt. Why?" Pru asked.

"You were grunting and groaning like some old woman, that's why," said Janie, shaking and slapping her pant legs to rid herself of dirt and leaves.

Using the same procedure, Prudence was finally satisfied, but began slapping at Janie's back.

"Stop it Pru. I know I have leaves all over me, but you don't have to slap so hard."

The next morning the two friends met at the intersection of Ivy Road and Vine Street on their way to school. Willowdale Elementary and Middle School was only three blocks further along at the entrance to Willow Street and since First Grade the two friends had walked to and from school together.

"It looks like neither of us got caught" said Janie, smiling brightly. "You worried for nothing, didn't you, Pru?"

"Like Grandpa always says though, 'one of these days our luck will run out' and then we'll be in a mess," replied Pru.

Janie adjusted her backpack and fell into step beside Pru. "We'll have to go back, you know. The taller of the men said they'd have to bring whatever they were carrying back the same way."

"Go back! No, Janie. I'm not going back. That man that you said whispered sounded dangerous. I'm not going to take a chance on getting killed."

Janie stopped and grabbed Pru's arm. "We're not going to let them see us, silly. We'll stay hid like we did last night."

Pru jerked her arm out of Janie's grasp. "I thought my heart would stop last night when they were close enough for me to hear a man talking. That's why I fainted. I'll bet a person could die if they got scared bad enough. Besides it isn't any of our business what they were doing. Let Kyle Jester tell his tall tales. If he's so afraid that something criminal is going on he can find out himself or call the police."

"Kyle just said that he'd heard his dad say that several businesses were missing some of their goods and then Henry Mercer said that several people had reported seeing lights in the cemetery at night. I tied the two together and I just know we saw, no not really saw, but we did hear the crooks last night. But Pru, we don't have to go after dark tonight. I don't believe they'll be back tonight, but I do want to find out where they came from. There's a stone wall around three sides of the cemetery and I don't think they lifted that big crate or box over that stone wall, do you? They had to get in the cemetery some way, though."

"They went out through the gate so they probably came in before we got there," said Pru as if Janie should have known that.

"That tall man said that he'd rather be there in the cemetery as down there. Now, what did he mean, 'down there?' said Janie with a puzzled scowl.

"I don't care what he meant and I don't plan to find out. That whispering man that scared you would scare me to death. I'd probably die instead of faint if I'd heard him," said Pru and shivered.

"Well, you just fainted, but you were as heavy as a dead person. You started sliding toward the ground and I couldn't let you fall. A noise like that would have got us in trouble for sure."

They had now arrived at school and their guessing at clues had to be put on hold until the evening.

CHAPTER 2

Janie and Pru were both in the seventh grade even though Janie was several months older than Pru. "My birthday is in October and I couldn't start to school until I was almost seven. That's the reason you are in my grade, Pru. I don't know where you got the idea that you are smarter than I am."

Janie glared in annoyance. "You know I have to help you with all your math homework."

"Yes, but I help you with your writing assignments. You can't spell cat."

"You didn't have to laugh your head off when I spelled fatigue wrong in English class. I don't tell anybody that you can't add two and two," scolded Janie.

Pru laughed. "Well it was funny and I can laugh if I want to." Pru flung her head up, her bob of curly red hair bouncing indignantly. Their arguments, on a daily basis, didn't change their habits of best buddies. They still walked side by side on their way to science class.

Their science teacher this year, Miss Cross, was a slender, cheerful, young woman with glasses, short blond hair and bangs. She wore knee-high boots and short plaid skirts with long pullover sweaters that fell to two inches above the hem of her skirts. She had sharp, penetrating eyes and her glasses gave her the appearance of seeing everything at once. The first morning they all filed into the classroom, she sat down on a tall stool and stared until every student was in the room.

"I am M. K. Cross, your science teacher this year. Find a seat. Sit down and be quiet. I need to get your names and learn something about each of you. I don't like working with strangers," were her first words.

Janie loved her immediately. "Miss Cross, why are you wearing boots? It's fall not winter."

Miss Cross looked at her sternly. "Please raise your hand and ask permission before speaking. I wear boots because I like boots. Why do you wear a denim jacket? It's too hot in this weather."

Janie grinned but didn't reply to her question.

Miss Cross gave Janie a saucy grin and raised her eyebrows and then starting on the right side of the room she began. Pointing to Mary Fletcher, who was seated in the front seat, she said, "What is your name? What are the names of your parents? What is your address and telephone number?" Then, one by one, she wrote down names, addresses, and anything else the student wanted to tell her.

Janie raised her hand and asked, "What if someone doesn't want to tell you anything else?"

"I'm not forcing anyone."

Finally she came to Janie. "Janie Query. Hm-m-m, your name is certainly appropriate. I mean your last name of course, since you always question everything."

Janie looked at her. "How will I learn anything, if I don't ask? I guess I just like to learn."

"Maybe, or maybe you just like attention," said Miss Cross.

Janie sat back as if thinking. "No, I don't think it's that. I just always want to know why or how something is the way it is. People say I'm curious. Well, some just say I'm nosey, but I don't think I am."

Miss Cross shook her head. "Well, I can't help what you think, but you are getting a lot of attention. That isn't fair to the other students. I'm sure you want to be fair, don't you, Miss Query?

"Yes, I do. I'm sorry." Janie's face turned red as she looked around and saw her classmates hiding their grins.

Kyle Jester sniggered loud enough to be heard and gained the attention Miss Cross accused Janie of wanting.

Miss Cross looked down her list. "Mr. Jester…Kyle, do you want to share your joke?"

Janie looked at Kyle with a satisfied smirk. *Good for you, Mr. Jester. I'm sure you didn't expect that,* she thought.

"Well, we're waiting. What was so amusing?" asked Miss Cross.

Kyle squirmed in his seat. "It was just seeing Janie's face when you embarrassed her. She looked funny."

Miss Cross abruptly swung her eyes toward Janie. "There's another adjective you can add to your description, Miss Query. Does that one fit your personality as well?"

Janie raised her shoulders in a shrug. "I don't know, Miss Cross. I guess we'll just have to wait and see."

Miss Cross rolled her eyes and turned to the front of the room where the chalkboard was and began to write.

Janie drew no more attention that day. Miss Cross was very creative in her approach to teaching science and often drew pictures and designs to pen-point various points she wanted to make. This day it was about the food chains of various amphibians. All the students paid close attention and Janie became so engrossed that she didn't hear the bell.

"Come on Janie. Didn't you hear the bell?" Prudence yanked at her arm and Janie jerked around in surprise.

"What? I think I've figured out why the tadpoles thrive best in ponds. Is it time to go?"

"Look around you, silly. We're the last ones here," said Pru turning toward the door. Janie quickly put her folder and pencils together, grabbed her backpack, and followed Pru into the hall. Miss Cross was coming from the office and Janie smiled and said, "Bye, Miss Cross."

Miss Cross smiled. "Bye Curious Janie Query," then shook her head and went into her room.

"Miss Cross likes you, Janie," said Pru as they hurried down the steps and onto the sidewalk.

"I like her too. She's smart. Don't you think she's smart?"

Prudence shook her head as if amazed. "Of course she's smart. She's the teacher."

"Mr. Ratliff is a teacher, but I don't think he's smart," said Janie thoughtfully. "Do you think he's smart, Pru?"

Prudence walked on and didn't answer.

"I won't tell anybody that you said he wasn't smart, but you know that we both went to sleep in his history class last year," stated Janie firmly as they stopped for the light.

Once the light changed, Janie asked again. "Well, do you think Mr. Ratliff is smart, Pru?"

"I –I think he probably knows a lot about history, but he's not good at teaching it," said Pru thoughtfully.

They walked a little farther. "You're pretty smart, Pru. I didn't know you were such a deep thinker."

"I'm not, but I kind of feel sorry for Mr. Ratliff. I hope he never hears the kids calling him 'Mr. Ratty.' I don't like to hurt people's feelings, do you," asked Pru, stopping to look at Janie.

Janie grinned. "I'm not supposed to be a deep thinker. I'm just curious."

Pru giggled and pushed her between the shoulders. "I don't know about people, but you don't like to hurt animals. We both know that. You almost got us both killed trying to climb that giant tree to get Mrs. Taylor's cat down."

Janie laughed. "She didn't even thank us either. I guess she was afraid we'd sue for damages when her cat scratched us to pieces."

They were still laughing when they reached the Ivy Road turn-off that led to Pru's house. "Pru, I'll call you after we eat. That will give us time to get to the cemetery and get home before dark," said Janie.

"I don't really want to go back there, Janie. What if those men are there?"

"They'll just think we're there to decorate. I'll take a bunch of flowers," said Janie. Pru still did not look convinced and Janie made it worse with her next comment.

"I hope those men are there. Then we'd have a good look at two men that carry heavy loads through a cemetery at night."

Prudence stood obstinately looking down. "That makes it worse. If they saw us looking at them they'd get suspicious. Now, I'm really afraid to go. It's too dangerous. Why don't you tell your brother, Jimmy, and let him investigate?"

Janie drew in a long exasperated breath. "Pru, Pru, you know what he'll say even before I ask."

Pru grinned. "I can just hear him now. 'Janie, Janie, You never learn do you? That Jester boy knows how to get you going, doesn't he?'"

Janie laughed. "You sound just like Jimmy, but your voice isn't quite as deep. He always thinks I listen to made-up stories and believe them, but I don't."

"Yes you do. I'm not going back to that cemetery today no matter what you say." Prudence gave Janie a stubborn glare.

Janie frowned and dropped her head in disappointment. "Well, I'd like to have you with me, but I can go by myself. Bye, Pru. See you tomorrow." Janie turned away and started on down Vine Street toward her house, only to be jerked around.

"You know I won't let you go by yourself, so call me

and we'll meet at the cemetery gates," said Pru with a 'we may get killed but you're my friend' look.

"No, no, Pru. You don't want to go. I'll be fine," said Janie, but she looked sad.

Pru grabbed her shoulders. "Are we friends or not? If we're friends then I'm going with you, so you better be at that gate at five-thirty."

Janie grinned and threw her arms around Pru. Pru pushed her away. "You're just hugging me because you got your way."

Janie stood grinning. "Okay friend. See you there." Janie adjusted her backpack to a more comfortable position and turned toward home.

Prudence looked back when she heard Janie singing, 'I'm a Yankee Doodle Dandy' which Pru knew was Janie's happy song.

"If those men are there she'll be singing another tune, I'll bet," mumbled Pru and swung around to head down Ivy Street.

CHAPTER 3

Janie was standing at the cemetery gate, holding a vase with a beautiful floral arrangement of artificial carnations and gladiolas when Pru arrived.

"That's your mother's newest arrangement, Janie. Mom was with her when she bought it at the Farmers Market just this week. She'll kill you for taking it. She puts new flowers on that table in front of the dining room window every month." said Pru, thinking about how nice they looked when she passed Janie's house.

"She's not ready to change the flowers yet and I'm going to take them back. I couldn't find any more flowers that weren't out on tables." Janie turned to the gate and lifted the latch. The gate creaked ominously and Pru shivered.

"Pru, why are you shivering? It's broad daylight and I can't hear a sound except the birds, can you?"

"No." Pru stood quiet, listening. "I can't hear anything,

so let's do whatever it is you want to do and go home." Pru hurried through the gate but left it open. Janie didn't notice this and went happily up the low slant, which leveled out to seemingly miles of tombstones of various sizes and shapes.

When they reached the huge oak tree that they both called "Grandpa's Oak," they stopped to look around. Janie went behind the tree and stood for a moment.

She pointed to the right. "They came this way, so look closely at everything we pass and look for footprints. We're bound to see something."

The girls began a slow step by step inspection of the tombstones and the ground around them as they made their way toward the rock wall which enclosed the cemetery's outer border. They had gone about twenty feet when Pru suddenly stopped.

"Look at this Janie. It looks like something scrubbed the side of this stone, doesn't it"

Janie dropped to her knees to study it, then suddenly gasped. "Pru, look what I've found." She held up a piece of paper. It wasn't just any paper, though.

Pru took the paper from her hand. "This is part of a dollar bill, isn't it?"

"I don't know whether it's a dollar bill, or a five dollar bill, but it is a torn scrap from some kind of paper money." Janie put the scrap in her jacket pocket and looked all around.

"What are you looking for now?"

"I'm making sure I'll know where we found this." Janie walked to the front of the grave and knelt down in front of the stone marker. "Eliza Marie Hanasett. Can you remember that name, Pru?"

"Oh E-Li-za, little Li-za Jane," hummed Pru. "Yeah, I'll remember her first name and Marie is my middle name, so I can remember both those names."

Suddenly she clapped her hands together and laughed. "There, now I can remember all three names—E-Li-za, my middle name, and hands for Hannaset."

Janie grinned. "So that's how you do so well on tests. When you want to remember something you link it with something you already know. That's real sharp, Pru."

Pru laughed. "A good memory is very useful, especially on tests."

Janie rose from her knees and brushed the dirt from her jeans. "Well, I guess they came this way, so let's see what else we can find."

They made a meticulous search for ten or twelve more feet before Janie abruptly stopped. "Pru, look at this! This stone has been moved or something. See the grass, dirt, and leaves that have recently been heaped up around it at the bottom. Why would anybody do that?"

Pru turned pale." I don't know Janie. Let's go home. I don't want to find out why anyone would dig around a tombstone."

Janie went around to the front again and bent down to see the name. "William (Big Boy) Jackson. What a strange name. I guess Big Boy was his nickname, don't you"

Suddenly they heard voices over near the gate. Pru looked at Janie, her eyes wide with fear. "What'll we do?"

"We'll go right back to the gate and leave." Pru, where did I leave that pot of flowers? I need the flowers to explain why we're here."

"You must have set them down…I know. You left them with Eliza Marie Hannasett," said Pru with a mischievous grin.

Janie grinned too. "We'd better go visit Miss Hannasett hadn't we?"

They quickly walked back the way they had come and as they neared Eliza's grave they saw a man and two women standing by a grave not too far away.

Janie whispered. "I have to take these flowers back or Mom will be asking every neighbor if they've seen someone with her flowers." Janie picked up the flowers and stood for a moment.

"I know. We're trying to find a great aunt who is supposed to be buried here."

Janie grabbed up the flowers and taking the lead she walked slowly, looking to the right and left. When they approached the other visitors, they stopped.

"Hello. Are you visiting a relative's grave?" Janie smiled. "We have been trying to find my great aunt's grave, but with no luck."

"Aren't you two girls afraid to come to a cemetery alone? Most young people couldn't be hired to come here," said the older woman.

"Why would they be afraid? Dead people can't hurt anybody. We… I think it's peaceful here, don't you?" Janie asked, looking at the man.

He looked around. "Yes, I suppose, but it's kind of sad. I mean it can't be a happy place to visit for you girls."

Pru blurted out. "We're not just visiting. We're looking

for…" She didn't finish since Janie stepped back onto her foot.

"We're looking for my Aunt Arbutus' grave. I wanted to put flowers on it if we found it," said Janie, holding up the flowers.

The young woman smiled. "How sweet!"

"What's her last name?" asked the older woman.

"M-Macintosh. Arbutus Matilda Macintosh," said Janie and wondered where that name came from.

"There's some Macintoshes right back over there," said the man, pointing to the right of the gate.

Inwardly sighing in relief, Janie said, "Thanks! I'll bet that's where she's buried." Both girls turned to go in that direction to be stopped.

"Is the gate kept closed? It was standing open as we came in," said the young woman.

Janie looked at Pru. "That's strange! It is always closed when we come by here."

"You forgot to shut the gate, didn't you?"

"I did not," said Pru, looking toward the gate.

"You must have. I was in front and I was carrying the flowers," said Janie as they moved farther away from the visitors.

The man laughed and yelled. "Don't quarrel about it. We'll close it when we leave."

The two girls walked toward the right of the gate with heads turning from right to left as if searching for something. Janie suddenly stopped. "Pru, we should have asked whose grave they were visiting. Let's go back and ask them."

"Go back and ask them! Why do we want to do that?

They'll just think we're nosey, which you are, but I'm not," said Pru stubbornly.

Janie turned back and soon came up to the man. "We should have asked who your relative was. We may know where the grave is."

The man jerked around nervously. "Thank you, but we've given up. We've come to the wrong cemetery. We knew the grave was on the north side and none of the tombstones we were told about are here."

The two women who had been a few yards away came up at that time and looked at the girls curiously. The man said, "Mother, I've just told these young ladies that we've mistakenly come to the wrong cemetery. They've come to help us search. Isn't that nice of them?"

The older woman smiled. "Yes, it is. Thanks girls, but we're ready to leave. Did you find your aunt…Arbutus Matilda McIntosh's grave?"

The two girls were stunned for a moment. The aunt's name had gone out of their minds. Janie, however, recovered quickly and said, "No, we didn't complete our search since we felt you people were strangers and we might be of help."

The young woman smiled widely. "You girls are just the sweetest things. If we hadn't discovered this was the wrong cemetery we would have appreciated your help."

Pru pinched Janie's arm. "I guess we'll finish our search then. Good-bye." Pru turned with Janie's arm still tingling from the pinch, and grasping her shirt tail, started walking away.

Janie smiled and said good-bye as well and followed Pru back the way they had come.

When they were out of earshot of the strangers they both stopped. “Well, Miss Curious Janie Query, you didn’t learn anything that time, did you?”

Janie shook her head then giggled. “Yes I did. I learned that you can pinch harder than you could last year and I learned that the older woman has a very good memory.”

“Yes she does. I was shocked when she said Arbutus, but then it all came back to me.” They heard voices and looked back to see the two women and the man walking toward the gate.

They immediately stooped as if reading the names on the various tombstones and kept at it until they saw the strangers going through the gate.

“We should have asked their names. Boy, how stupid can we be? Now we’ll never know what they were doing here.” Janie stomped her foot in disgust.

“They came to the wrong cemetery, Janie. They told us that.”

“Pru, this is the only cemetery in this town. If they came to the wrong cemetery they also came to the wrong town. That does not make a bit of sense, does it?”

Pru shrugged her shoulders. “They looked intelligent, so they must have known what town they were in, don’t you think.”

Janie grimaced. “I think they acted strange and I don’t think they were telling the truth either.”

Pru looked west at the setting sun. “Unless we want to be here after dark we need to go, so come on.”

Janie grabbed up the flowers and followed Pru out and this time made sure the gate was closed.

CHAPTER 4

During breakfast the next morning Janie asked, "Is the Garden of Eternal Peace the only cemetery in this town?"

"Yes, it is," answered her father, folding his newspaper. "Why do you ask?"

"Pru and I met some people yesterday that were looking for somebody's grave, but they said they had come to the wrong cemetery. They looked like smart people, so that just made me wonder."

Jimmy came in just then, pulled out a chair, and sat down at the table. "What's to wonder about them going to the wrong cemetery? Lots of people go to the wrong addresses."

Janie's eyes widened. "Well, if they knew anything about the town of Willowdale, they certainly should have known that it has only one cemetery."

"What did they look like? They may be people that once lived here and moved away," said Mrs. Query, also taking a seat at the table.

"No, that won't do. If they had once lived here they would know that we only have one cemetery, wouldn't they, Dad?" asked Jimmy.

"I would think so, but they could have been tracing their genealogy and just knew they had someone buried in Willowdale."

Janie finished her cereal and rose from her seat. "I guess you're right, Dad. I have to go. Pru will be waiting on me at the crossroads." She hugged her mother and then her dad and said, "Bye, Jimmy" as she went out the kitchen door.

"Wait just a minute, young lady," said her mother, standing with the kitchen door open. "Where did you see these people and when did you see them?"

Janie stopped and slowly turned around. "I saw them yesterday afternoon when I went to play with Pru. Remember, I told you I was going to meet Pru."

Mrs. Query stood a moment longer and then said, "Well, bye. Have a good day."

Janie hurried away very thankful that she didn't have to lie to her mother. When she arrived at the Ivy Road intersection, Pru was waiting and the first thing Janie said was, "Mom wanted to know where we saw those people yesterday evening."

"Janie! You didn't tell her we'd been to the cemetery did you?"

"Well, duh! Of course I didn't tell her we were at the cemetery."

"I'm glad you didn't for if she knows, she'll tell Mom and I won't get to go to the carnival." Pru glared at Janie.

"Don't get all upset. I didn't tell her we met them at the cemetery, Pru. I just told her we saw them when we were playing."

"You mean she didn't ask where we were playing."

"No, but she asked where we met those people, and I hope she forgets all about it. I don't want to lie to my mother," said Janie with a worried frown.

"Why did you mention meeting anyone? Are you stupid? Janie, you know that moms want to know who you met and what they looked like, and...Well, you know that she won't forget it. Mine certainly wouldn't. I didn't mention it to my mom." Pru gave Janie an outraged stare as they fell into step together.

Janie shrugged her shoulders. "I didn't just go in and tell Mom. I asked Dad if there is more than one cemetery in Willowdale. That's what brought the subject up."

They walked on to the light and stood waiting. "I don't know why you wanted to know that. We won't see those people anymore."

Janie stopped. "Don't you ask somebody when you want to know something? I do, and I thought they acted funny."

"Your kind of thinking is going to cause me to miss the carnival. You know how much I like carnivals," said Pru with such a sad look that Janie was upset.

"Come on, Pru. Don't be sad. Maybe Mom will forget about it." Janie threw her arm around Pru's shoulders.

Pru sighed. "No, I may as well forget it. Our moms

will get together and we'll both be grounded for weeks." Pru's voice was so gloomy that Janie felt awful.

"I'm sorry, Pru. I only asked that one question, but when Jimmy came in, it turned into a family discussion. If it comes out that we were at the cemetery, I'll tell Aunt Audrey that I begged you to go and you couldn't turn me down. She'll believe that since she knows me."

"Yeah, we all know you, Janie Query, and Mom will say, 'Pru, you know better than to follow Janie when she gets a wild idea in her head. You're grounded, young lady. I've told you time and time again not to do whatever Janie asks, but you did it anyway. I can't trust you anymore.'" Pru was on the verge of tears.

Janie stopped and Pru stopped with her. "Okay, Pru. I'm sorry and I promise, if we are asked, I'll explain the entire thing. I don't want to hurt you."

They had reached the school grounds and had to drop their discussion, but it stayed in both their minds.

Both girls started home that evening feeling they were walking into a storm. "I don't know how, Pru, but I promise that I'll make them understand that none of this was your idea. You just went along so I wouldn't be by myself." Janie walked on for a few steps and turned. "That's the truth, too."

"They'll all believe that. They know that I'm a coward and would never have suggested going to a cemetery. In fact, I don't know how you talked me into going with you," said Pru.

Janie grinned. "You went because I'm your best friend and you know I'd do the same for you."

Pru nodded in agreement and walked stoically on beside her friend. Suddenly she stopped. "Janie, I wouldn't ask you to go to a cemetery after dark, and I wouldn't ask you to climb a giant tree to get a cat down. I just don't think about doing all the things you want to do."

Janie patted her shoulder consolingly. "I know, Pru, but we do have lots of adventures don't we?"

"We probably won't after this deal. That might be a good thing, too."

"You shouldn't be stopped from going to the carnival, Pru, and neither should I. I wonder if our parents ever thought that you and I should be allowed to be involved in more things like carnivals, fairs, and races. I guess they have forgotten that 'idle hands are the devil's workshop' and that you and I need to keep our minds stimulated."

The girls had reached the intersection of Ivy Road and Vine Street and come to a dead stop. Janie turned to Pru.

"I think that argument might work, don't you? I mean we can say we investigate things because it stimulates our minds. Well, don't just stand there. Say something, Pru."

Pru looked at Janie solemnly and shook her head. "They may think that of you, Janie, but they certainly won't think that of me." Pru let out a long sigh. "Let's just face it. The carnival is out and maybe a lot of other things."

Janie suddenly grasped Pru's shoulders and turned her around. "Don't give up hope. Something may happen before we have to tell. Let's just go home and try to forget about it."

Pru shrugged her shoulders. "We can try, but we both know that it won't work."

They parted, each going toward their own homes. They didn't skip along the road, however. As Janie's Grandpa would have said, 'they went at a snail's pace.'

When Janie rounded the curve, just as their house came into view, she stopped in surprise.

"Aunt Tabby!" she yelled and broke into a run.

Tabitha Martin, her father's sister, visited 'out-of-the-blue' anytime during the year and her station-wagon was parked before the house.

The snail's pace was forgotten as Janie sprinted the next four hundred feet and jumped up the steps to the front porch.

"Aunt Tabby! Aunt Tabby!" She yelled as she jerked open the door.

Soon she was gathered in plump, loving arms. "Stand back, girl! Let me look at you." Aunt Tabby walked around Janie and stopped back in front of her.

"You're just as curious as ever. What kind of adventure are you having now?"

Janie walked around her aunt and stopped back in front of her. She grinned and raised her eyebrows. "You're chubbier than ever. What kind of diet are you on now?"

Aunt Tabby chuckled. "I'm not dieting, as you can tell, but I may before I leave here. You look great and I'm glad to see you."

Janie threw her arms around her aunt again and kissed her cheek. "Oh I'm so glad to see you, Aunt Tabby. This is better than a Christmas present."

Arm in arm they walked through the living room, stopping for Janie to drop her backpack behind the door.

As they walked into the kitchen Aunt Tabby said, "Look what I caught creeping into your house."

Mr. Query turned from the stove with a bowl of creamed potatoes. "We'll feed her too, so gather around the table."

Janie didn't think about the cemetery and neither did anyone else that evening. Tabitha Query Martin was always welcomed with open arms even though she dropped in without any warning.

Mrs. Query had often said, "I'd send anyone else packing that showed up at my door without even a phone call, but not Tabby. Tabby, well…she's…she's a grown-up Janie."

"We never know what to expect from Tabby, that's for certain. Remember the time she brought that monkey to Jimmy and it almost destroyed our entire house," said Mr. Query and Mrs. Query broke into a merry laugh.

Mr. Query looked and Janie and chuckled also. "It's funny now, but I don't remember you laughing then."

"I laughed, but I didn't like it when he pulled my braid. I thought he was going to jerk my head off," said Janie.

"You were little then. You know, Dad that could account for the wild things Janie does now, couldn't it?" Jimmy laughed and jerked at Janie's pigtail.

Later when the Query family went to bed, Janie thought. "Well, I told Pru something might happen and it has. They'll all be so happy to see Aunt Tabby that they won't think about a cemetery as long as she's here."

CHAPTER 5

Aunt Tabby showed up on Wednesday and Saturday was the carnival, so the two girls spent a happy week at school and also at home. The Leery family came to a cookout held by the Query family on Friday and they all agreed to take the girls to the carnival on Saturday.

Pru looked at Janie, who smiled and raised her eyebrows as if saying, "See, I told you something would happen." This made her look more curious than ever since it brought her eyebrows closer to her hairline and the white streak seemed to begin at the top rim of her glasses.

Saturday morning was ushered in by bright sunshine and a clear blue sky. Janie hurried down stairs and ran to the kitchen door. "Oh great! This is a perfect day for a carnival, isn't it, Mom?"

Mrs. Query was standing on the kitchen deck savoring

her first cup of coffee. "Looks like it, but it may get hot. You may have to leave off your "Denim" jacket."

"Why are you stressing 'Denim,' Mary Ann?" asked her sister-in-law as she stepped through the kitchen door.

"Janie hasn't been out of that jacket except to sleep since you sent it last Christmas. I have to wash it after she goes to bed." Mary Ann Query rolled her eyes at Janie who had already donned her denim jacket.

"Aunt Tabby sent me this jacket and I like it." She looked at her aunt and smiled. "I like Aunt Tabby too." Janie threw her arms around her aunt who jerked back with her arm high in the air.

"Oops! Did I burn you? I spilled coffee on your jacket. Here, let me see."

Aunt Tabby looked so sad. "I guess you can't wear your jacket today, Janie. It's all stained with coffee."

"Rats! I'll feel naked without my jacket. I'd better call Pru. She only wears hers because I do. If I don't tell her, she'll thump me good." Janie went back into the kitchen.

The two women took chairs on the porch and sat sipping their coffee. "She gets more like you every day, Tabby. She should have been your child."

Tabby smiled sadly. "Maybe the Lord made her like me, since I'll never have a child of my own."

She again smiled, but with a mischievous gleam. "I'll bet you wish she was like Thelma instead of me, don't you?"

"No. I like Thelma, but of all of John's people I feel closest to you." Mary Ann Query rose from her chair and turned toward the kitchen door. She held the door for Tabby to follow her into the house.

Once she was inside she looked back at Tabby and said, "I guess you know that all that praise was to insure that you are the responsible party when we take the girls to the carnival."

Janie was seated at the kitchen table. "I hope Aunt Tabby does hang out with me and Pru. You and Aunt Audrey always want to try to win those cheap stuffed animals."

Tabby and Mary Ann laughed. "Aunt Audrey and I like to bring home something to show for all the money we spend at those places."

Soon Mr. Query and Jimmy entered the kitchen and took their seats. "What's for breakfast, Mom?" Jimmy asked, as he turned to look at his father."I wish you had made pancakes, Dad. Why didn't you?"

"Oh no, not today. I did the grilling last night."

"You'll eat eggs, bacon, and toast, young man, and you'd better not utter one complaint." Mrs. Query gave Jimmy a gimlet look. "Somebody may want to borrow my car."

Everybody looked at Jimmy. They all knew he had a date for that evening.

That statement was like an off switch for Jimmy and no other comments were made about breakfast. Soon Mrs. Query pushed her chair back from the table and looked around at everyone.

"Everybody go right ahead and rush away. Before you do though, rake your plates in the garbage disposal. I hate to see five eggs thrown away, but either I'm a bad cook or everybody is in a rush." She looked around the table and smiled as she pointed to her own plate. "I didn't want eggs either."

All the females piled into Aunt Tabby's Subaru station wagon leaving Mr. Query, Jimmy, and Mr. Leery to ride in Mr. Query's Ford Explorer. Both vehicles reached the carnival at the same time and found parking spaces beside each other. Mr. Query stepped out of his vehicle and looked around.

"Looks like everybody in the county is here, so keep an eye on your wallets or whatever you girls carry."

"Tabby, keep your eye on the girls as well as their money. Why don't you girls just give your money to Aunt Tabby? It'll be safer with her," said Mrs. Query.

"No, it won't. Somebody could grab it from her hand and run. Look at her. Could she outrun me and Pru?" Janie asked.

Automatically every head turned toward Aunt Tabby and then smiles were on every face. "You have a point, Janie, but will Aunt Tabby be hanging upside down on the rides?"

"No, she won't," said Aunt Tabby. "You girls take care of your own money. I might spend it if I see something I want."

The others laughed and then parted company, each group going in its chosen direction.

Aunt Tabby rode some rides with Janie and Pru. She liked the Ferris wheel and the Merry-Go-Round, but not the Tilt-a-Whirl and the Silver Bullet.

"Girls, I just can't ride things that have me almost bottom up. I get deathly sick on those things. I'll sit here and wait for you. Go ahead and get your tickets," said Aunt Tabby, who had stopped to buy a wide-brimmed straw hat. Placing the hat on her head at a jaunty angle she made her way to a bench and sat down.

Pru and Janie walked perkily toward the other rides. When Janie climbed out of the Silver Bullet she was so disoriented that Pru had to steady her before they could pass through the barrier gate.

"Janie, you're white as a sheet. Are you sick?" asked an anxious Aunt Tabby.

Janie plopped down on the seat beside her aunt. "No, not really, but I guess I must be just like you, Aunt Tabby. I don't like to be bottom up either."

Aunt Tabby hugged her and said, "I think you'd better sit here for a bit before you tackle the Roller Coaster, don't you?"

"I'll go get us something to drink, Janie. Do you want anything else?" asked Pru before turning to Aunt Tabby. "What about you, Aunt Tabby?"

Aunt Tabby looked around. "Oh, I see a refreshment stand right over there. I don't want you to get too far away without me being with you."

She fished in her pocket and brought out some money. "Get me one of those iced pink lemonades please."

Pru hurried away, but Aunt Tabby kept her eyes right on her. "I'm glad she's wearing that bright orange shirt. It stands out a mile."

Janie sighed as the nausea wore off. "It sure is hot and crowded isn't it? Finding someone here would be like looking for a needle in a haystack."

"Worse than that, I'd think. People keep moving and milling about and about the time you have someone spotted a group will walk in front of them, then you never see them again," said Aunt Tabby, stretching up on her tiptoes, not wanting to lose sight of Prudence.

Pru came back with three pink iced lemonades and they sat sipping and relaxing. They were enjoying the spectacle of people in all forms of dress and of all nationalities.

"Those women with the dresses that look like a long piece of cloth draped around them, are from India, aren't they?" asked Pru. They all looked with interest at a woman holding a pretty child. She was draped in material and had a marquise cut stone on her forehead that was attached to a scarf covering her head.

"She's from India, Pakistan, or maybe Ceylon, I think. She's very pretty isn't she?" Aunt Tabby smiled at the woman, and the woman shyly smiled and quickly dropped her head.

Janie plucked at Aunt Tabby's sleeve and whispered. "I don't think they are supposed to look directly at people, especially strangers. It may be against one of their laws. That Muslim Sharia law is awfully strict especially on women."

Aunt Tabby shook her head. "If she's from any of the Indonesian countries she's probably Hindu. I don't know much about their laws."

"How come you know anything about Muslims, Janie? We've not studied anything about them yet," said Pru in a puzzled voice.

Janie rose from her seat and stretched. "I read a book about the Middle East, or at least about Pakistan and Afghanistan. I sure wouldn't want to live there."

"What book was that, Janie?" Aunt Tabby had also risen and now looked at Janie.

"Far, uh...Pavilions, by M. M. Kaye. It was thick and it took me a long time...almost all last summer when we went to the beach."

"I wouldn't read a book like that, would you, Aunt Tabby?" asked Pru but then became excited as the waiting line shortened for the Roller Coaster.

"Come on, Janie. Let's ride the Roller Coaster before we eat lunch," said Pru, turning in that direction. Arm in arm with Aunt Tabby in the middle they went weaving their way through the crowd.

They were passing a food pavilion when Janie suddenly spied their science teacher, Miss Cross. She was talking to some man, but Janie didn't let that deter her. She led the way with Pru and Aunt Tabby trailing her, and came to a stop in front of Miss Cross.

Janie plucked at her sleeve and Miss Cross turned a cross face toward her. "Oh, hello Curious..." she didn't get to finish, but was interrupted by the man.

He smiled and nodded. "Come see me next week," he said as he walked away. He spoke in a rough whisper which was hard to understand.

Janie gasped and turned deathly pale. Miss Cross blinked in fright. "Are you going to faint?"

CHAPTER 6

Janie realized that she was the only person there who had heard that voice before, but now she wasn't sure if it was the same voice. She tried to get control of herself by taking several big gulps of air. "I've never fainted in my life. Why would I want to faint?"

Miss Cross looked at her narrowly. "Well, people usually only look that white in their caskets."

Aunt Tabby bristled. "What a thing to say to a child? What kind of person are you?"

"Aunt Tabby, this is Miss Cross, our science teacher. She's nice," said Pru.

"A science teacher? I've never heard a teacher talk like that to a student in my life."

Miss Cross looked at Aunt Tabby. "Well, Janie is a curious girl. She likes plain talk and she did look like she was about to faint."

"She's still pale. I think we'd better sit down for a bit," said Aunt Tabby, grasping Janie's arm. Janie felt like her legs were wet spaghetti so she didn't move.

Miss Cross saw this and grasped Janie's other arm. "I'll hold this side, Mrs.... Aunt Tabby. She still looks awfully pale."

They made it into the food pavilion and found a table. Miss Cross motioned to a waiter. "Bring her a coke. She isn't feeling well."

Soon Janie was sipping coke, which she didn't like, but since it was supposed to settle her stomach, according to Miss Cross, she continued to sip it.

Finally Janie put the coke down on the table. "I wasn't about to faint. I was shocked."

"Shocked? What shocked you?" Aunt Tabby looked at her in amazement.

"I didn't see anything to shock you. What was it?" asked Pru.

Janie looked at Miss Cross. "Who was that man you were talking to?"

"Do you mean the man I was speaking with when you grabbed my sleeve?"

"Yes. Who is he?"

"He's a finance officer from Settlers Bank and Trust. Why?" Miss Cross had that narrow look in her eyes again.

"Is he a friend of yours?"

"No. I was asking him about some banking business. I'd never met him in my life, but he wore a badge with the bank's logo on it. Didn't you see that badge on his coat?"

Janie scuffed her foot along the floor as if trying to

make a decision. "Would you go sit in Aunt Tabby's car with us? There's something I need to discuss with some grown-up and I don't want anyone else to hear it."

Miss Cross was wary since she heard, every day, about Janie's penchant for adventures. "Why me? I may not like adventures," said Miss Cross.

Janie looked at Aunt Tabby. "This morning I'd decided to talk to Aunt Tabby, but now, I think I need to talk to you both."

Miss Cross looked at Aunt Tabby and smiled. "I'm game if you are."

Aunt Tabby grinned. "I've never worked with a science teacher before. This just may be fun."

Still walking on each side of Janie the four of them made their slow weaving way to the parking area.

"We'll roast in the car, Janie. Why can't we sit under a tree or something?" asked Pru.

Janie looked around. "Do you see any trees, Pru? Besides, I don't want anyone else to hear what I have to say."

"I'll start the engine and put on the air-conditioner," said Aunt Tabby as she opened the door. Janie got in the front passenger seat with Aunt Tabby across from her and behind Aunt Tabby sat Miss Cross with Pru across from her.

Aunt Tabby immediately started the engine and soon the air-conditioner was purring.

"Okay, Curious Janie Query, what's this all about?" asked Miss Cross.

Janie looked at Pru. "Pru, do you remember me

telling you about the man that whispered that night in the Garden of Eternal Peace?"

Pru's eyes opened wide. "Did you see him again?"

"No, I didn't see him, but the man talking to Miss Cross whispered. The sound wasn't exactly like the man made when he talked, but it was enough like it to shock me."

Now, Pru turned pale and whispered, "Do you mean, he…he was the man helping to carry that box?"

"What are you girls talking about? The Garden of Eternal Peace is our local cemetery," said Aunt Tabby, turning to Miss Cross.

"We know that, Aunt Tabby, but wait until you hear the rest of what has happened." Janie sat up very straight and looked at Aunt Tabby and then back at Miss Cross.

Pru jumped in. "Janie has to investigate everything and Kyle Jester told us one day that his dad said that several businesses had been losing things. Of course Janie was curious about that, but she didn't do anything until a week later when Henry Mercer said that people had been seeing lights in the cemetery at night."

Now, Aunt Tabby sat up straight. "Janie, you went to the cemetery to investigate didn't you?"

Janie nodded her head. "Pru went with me and when she fainted I thought we'd get caught. I had to hold her up and keep us both hidden until they got past our tree."

"Until who got past? Who else was in the cemetery? It wasn't dark was it?" Now they had Miss Cross's attention.

Janie went on to tell about seeing two men carrying a long box up the little slope on the right. "It must have been heavy. They were grunting and moving slowly. They stopped right in front of the tree where we were hidden and Pru fainted."

Aunt Tabby looked at Miss Cross. "No wonder she fainted. I can't believe that you two little girls went to a cemetery alone after dark."

Miss Cross didn't seem to think that strange, however. "Where did they take this box? They didn't just stop and stay there, did they?"

"No, they went on, but the front man was complaining all the way. The man who was carrying the other end of the box was the boss. At least, I thought he was, since he told the front man to keep his mouth shut. I saw the first man, or the bulk of him, but I only heard the voice of the second man. He had a voice which sounded almost like the man you were talking with, Miss Cross." Janie lapsed into silence and sat waiting.

"Well, I do declare! I've never heard of such goings on. An officer in a bank carrying a box in the cemetery at night. That's hard to believe," said Aunt Tabby.

"I'm not a liar, Aunt Tabby."

"Lord, Janie, I know you're not a liar. I just meant that it's hard to believe that an important man like that would do silly things like carrying a box in a cemetery."

Aunt Tabby looked at Pru and smiled, "So you fainted, did you? It wouldn't much of an adventure to you, was it?"

"I went back to the cemetery with Janie the next evening. We met two women and a man. Janie thought they were suspicious, but you know Janie. She's always seeing clues in everything," said Pru.

"What made you think those people were suspicious, Janie? What were they doing?" asked Miss Cross.

"They said they were looking for a relative's grave, but they didn't know that Willowdale only had one cemetery. It just seemed to me that anybody with any intelligence would have found that out before they started looking."

Aunt Tabby interrupted with, "What I'd like to know is why you were going back the next day? Didn't you get scared enough the first time?"

Janie shook her head in exasperation. "Aunt Tabby you know that there's a high rock wall around the cemetery except in the front near the road. Well, I know that too, and it made me wonder how they got in the cemetery with that box. That's why I wanted to go back. I wanted to see if I could find out where they came from."

"We found some things too, didn't we, Janie?"

"Not much."

"We found a scrap of a dollar bill, and a tombstone had been moved or something. Probably they stumbled into it with that heavy load. It was dark as a dungeon that night," said Pru.

Miss Cross gave Janie an intent stare. "Wait a minute. How did you see anything or anybody if it was that dark?"

"It wasn't that dark, especially when the moon came out. It would first be behind a cloud and then it would break through. That's when we saw the tall man with a slouch hat on his head. We couldn't see his face, so we couldn't pick him out in a line up, could we Pru? I'll never forget that guttural whisper though, not until my dying day," said Janie and shivered. "That's why I was shocked today. That man did sound a lot like that man."

They all sat quietly thinking about the situation. Finally Janie said, "That's why I'm telling you and Miss Cross, Aunt Tabby. The tall man said they'd have to come back the same way and I'd like to have you with me when they do. I hadn't thought about Miss Cross until I saw her talking to that man today."

"At first, I thought she knew him or he was a friend, but when he left so quickly I didn't think she knew him very well." Janie looked at Miss Cross.

Miss Cross shook her head. "No, I just saw his logo and decided to see if he could help me on this financial arrangement I want to make."

"Will you and Aunt Tabby go with us to the cemetery tomorrow night? We need to go before nine o'clock and may have to wait around for a while," explained Janie.

Both women sat very still for a moment. Miss Cross looked at Aunt Tabby and grinned. "We may live to regret this, but I'll go if you will."

Aunt Tabby smiled and put out her hand. "Let's shake on it, partner."

CHAPTER 7

When the other members of the party arrived they found Janie, Pru, Aunt Tabby, and a young woman they didn't know, sitting in Aunt Tabby's station wagon.

"What on earth are all of you doing in a hot car on a day like this? It's hot enough to roast marshmallows out here," said Mrs. Query.

"That's why we're in here," said Aunt Tabby as she opened her door. We've had the air-conditioning on."

Audrey Leery looked at Pru. "I thought you wanted to ride every ride they had and now I find you sitting in a hot car."

Mr. Query looked at Janie. "Aren't you going to introduce your friend?"

"She's not our friend. She's our science teacher," blurted Pru.

Mr. Query put out his hand. "How do you do, Miss…"

He looked pointedly at Janie who suddenly became very alert.

"Miss Cross, Dad. I'm sorry. I guess I'm not feeling as well as I thought."

Mrs. Query switched her eyes from Miss Cross to Janie. "Aren't you feeling well? What's wrong?"

"The rides made her sick, Mary Ann. After the Tilt-a-Whirl, I insisted that we all sit for a bit and Pru got us some lemonade. Then they were all set for the Roller Coaster," said Aunt Tabby.

"But we didn't…" begin Pru, but Miss Cross stepped in front of her.

"That's when they met me and we've been talking since then. You have a very interesting daughter, Mrs. Query."

Mrs. Cleery grinned. "Everybody in this town knows that. In case you don't know it yet, she is known as Curious Janie Query."

Miss Cross laughed. "Yes, I do know it. Everybody at school calls her 'Curious Janie Query'."

Mr. Query raised his eyebrows and nodded. "To her that's a badge of honor."

"Well, it is a badge of honor, John. What would this world be like if there was no curiosity?" Aunt Tabby nodded her head vigorously as if everyone should have thought of that already.

John Query held up his hands, palms out, and backed up a step. "Whoa! Don't go ballistic, Tabby. I'm only teasing your godchild."

Pru's mother had stood during this exchange looking

puzzled. “I still don’t understand why all of you are sitting in a car? I know you have air-conditioning, but it takes gas to run an engine.”

“We wanted to talk, Mom, and Aunt Tabby volunteered to start the engine, didn’t you, Aunt Tabby?” Pru looked at her mother warily. “I don’t want you to blame me, if she runs out of gas.”

Aunt Tabby laughed. “Nobody’s blaming you, Pru. I can’t hear in all this noise and so we came to the car. I like to hear what’s being said.”

Mrs. Leery shrugged her shoulders. “It’s your dime, but I wouldn’t do it. I don’t need to hear anything that’s going to cost me money.” She laughed and so did the others.

“I’ll bet Miss Cross didn’t get to say much, did you, Miss Cross?” Mrs. Query asked with a smile.

Miss Cross smiled and got out of the car. “Oh yes. I had my say, but I have to hurry away right now. I have things to do.” She looked at Aunt Tabby and then Janie. She nodded her head and winked before smiling a slow smile. She then looked around at the others.

“It was nice to meet all of you. Now, I understand Janie…and Pru a lot better than I did.” This statement had the Query’s and the Leary’s exchanging puzzled looks, but they made no comments.

Miss Cross walked away with her boyish gait which seemed odd. She was small and looked dainty and frail but her gait said something else.

Soon they were all loaded into their cars. The two mothers wanted to hurry home and the two girls wanted to go into town. So, Aunt Tabby took only Janie and Pru in her station wagon.

"I'm certainly happy that we were lucky and didn't have to ride with Mary Ann and Pru's mother, aren't you, Janie?"

Janie was sitting across from Aunt Tabby, but was looking out the window. She turned her head. "Yes I am. Miss Cross was giving us some kind of sign, or at least, I thought she was. Let's go down Main Street. I think Miss Cross was going to the bank."

Aunt Tabby turned right out of the carnival grounds and soon was on Main Street. "She did give us a sign and we do need to see her. She doesn't know where nor when to meet us."

They drove slowly down the street. Janie was looking to the right where the bank was located. Suddenly Pru yelled. "There she is. She went in Sally's Boutique."

Aunt Tabby pulled to the curb and parked. "Okay, girls, let's go find some dresses or something," she said as she quickly wrenched open her door and stepped out.

They eagerly walked through the door thinking Miss Cross would be there in front. The shop wasn't large, and they soon realized that she wasn't there.

"There must be a back door somewhere. Let's ask the manager," said Janie heading for the cashier's desk.

Aunt Tabby grabbed her arm. "Wait, Janie. Look back in that corner. There's a curtain there. I'll bet it hides stairs or some kind of storage area, don't you?"

They walked back toward the curtain, stopping and examining items as they went. About the time they were ready to twitch the curtain aside, it parted and Miss Cross's head appeared. She smiled. "I thought you'd find me, but if you hadn't I was going back to school and get a phone number. Come on. I live upstairs."

They followed Miss Cross up narrow stairs that opened on a small landing. Miss Cross opened a door and they all stepped into a large, pleasant room that held living-room furniture, a bar with stools and kitchen appliances.

"I was born and raised in this town, but I had no idea this was up here. How did you find it?" asked Aunt Tabby.

"I had someone check out the town as to housing before I decided to take the job at Willowdale. I'm really pleased with this place. Nobody knows where I live and if it is told now, I'll know who to put the finger on."

Janie grinned. "Do you have a detective in your family?"

Miss Cross jerked her head around. "Why? Do I have to have in order to work with you? Why did you ask that anyway?"

"You used gangster talk…'put the finger on' and I just thought your dad or brother might be in law enforcement," said Janie.

Now Pru and Aunt Tabby had their eyes on Miss Cross. "Well, no, I don't have a detective in my family. However, I do know somebody who can help us should we need help. That information is also top secret."

"Pru and I know how to keep a secret, that's for sure and Aunt Tabby is as silent as the Buddha. She doesn't even tell our parents when we mess up unless we do something dangerous." Janie looked at Aunt Tabby and smiled.

"I don't usually know about the dangerous stuff until it's over with, young woman. That's a good thing, too. I'd probably have the police out looking for you every week," said Aunt Tabby.

Miss Cross motioned to the sofa and a chair. "Well, sit down and let's do some strategic planning." She went to the refrigerator and came back with a tray, holding lemonade and glasses, and put it on the coffee table.

By the time they'd all finished their lemonade; their plans for the following night were laid. Aunt Tabby checked her watch with Miss Cross's and leading the way, she, Janie, and Pru went down the stairs and one by one slipped around the curtain. They went back through the store looking at various things.

"Here, girls, how would you like to have one of these caps? See how they bulge out on the sides. One could put their hair up inside this and it would make a good disguise." Aunt Tabby put a dark brown one on and pushed her hair up under it. "See! With a checked shirt and without glasses I'd look different wouldn't I?"

"Okay, take your glasses off, Aunt Tabby," said Janie and stood with her hands on her hips.

"She doesn't look like Aunt Tabby, that's for sure." Pru took a dark green cap from the rack and soon had her hair hidden as well. "Go on Janie, get one."

Janie had been impressed by the change in Aunt Tabby's appearance. She took a dark blue cap from the rack and put it on her head, but her braids still hung down.

"Here, wind these braids around your head. You'll

never get then under the cap otherwise," said Aunt Tabby as she tried to coil the braids.

"Ouch! Let me do it, Aunt Tabby. You're pulling my eyeballs right out of my head." Janie circled her head with her braids and crammed the cap on over them.

"Take your glasses off, Janie," said Pru reaching to take Janie's glasses, but Janie pushed her hands away. "I'm not taking off my glasses. I can't see without them."

"You'll have to walk all bent over and take a cane with you then, unless you want someone to recognize you," said Pru.

"No, I'll have to do something else, but I do have to wear my glasses."

The caps were purchased and they left the store. On the sidewalk, Janie suddenly stopped. "I know we could be a club doing our initiation ritual."

"Why do we need to do that?" Pru was ready to get in the back seat since Aunt Tabby was unlocking her car.

"In case someone gets suspicious, Pru. It's always best to have a planned alibi. Isn't it Aunt Tabby?"

Aunt Tabby opened the door and turned to smile at Janie. "If you say so, Sherlock."

CHAPTER 8

The girls and Aunt Tabby arrived at the Query house just as dinner was being put on the table. Rubbing her hands together in anticipation, Aunt Tabby said, "Ah ha! Just in time. I'm hungry as a bear."

She turned to Janie with a questioning glare. "We did forget to eat lunch, didn't we?"

"Tabitha Martin! I can't believe you forgot lunch. You've been the first to the table all your life." Mr. Query looked skeptical and shook his head. "I believe age is getting to you, old girl."

Aunt Tabby raised her eyebrows. "I know. I can't believe it either." Again she turned to Janie and Pru. "We really didn't eat, did we?"

"No, Aunt Tabby, we didn't eat. Remember, I got sick, and you sent Pru to get us a lemonade and then we had a…All we've had today was lemonade. Let me behind the table. I knew I was really hungry for some reason." Janie started behind the table.

"No you don't, young lady. You wash your hands before you sit down at my table." Mary Ann Query stood glaring at the three late-comers.

Janie turned toward the bathroom and so did Pru and Aunt Tabby. "I washed my hands at M…," said Janie and Aunt Tabby laughed but gave Janie a warning glare.

"So did I, but Mary Ann has always been persnickety."

"I heard that Tabitha Martin." Mary Ann, Audrey Leery, and the others laughed when Aunt Tabby made a face in their direction.

The food was either delicious or they were all really hungry as evidenced by the empty bowls and platters when they arose from the table.

"I feel like I need a nap." John Query stretched his arms above his head and worked his shoulders right and left. "Anybody else for a nap?"

Aunt Tabby yawned, but looked at Janie. "I'm just yawning. I'm not going to take a nap."

"Why don't you, Tabby? I know these girls have worn you out." Mary Ann Query gave her a sympathetic look.

Aunty Tabby widened her eyes. "You're talking like I'm old, but I'm not. I can keep up with these two any day." She put her arm around Janie on one side and Pru on the other and they walked onto the kitchen patio.

Janie whispered softly. "Aunt Tabby, if you want to take a nap I can wake you when it's time to leave." Aunt Tabby looked at her watch.

"A ten minute nap wouldn't be near enough, so let's just get the things we need together."

Mary Ann Query put her head through the doorway. "I'm going to run Audrey out to the Farmers Market. You girls behave yourselves while I'm gone."

"Mom, we're going on a hike with Aunt Tabby and Miss Cross so we won't be here when you get back. Tell Aunt Audrey that Pru is going with us," said Janie.

Mrs. Query looked thoughtful. "As long as your Aunt Tabby is with you, but don't stay out too late."

When they heard the car drive away they went into a huddle. "We'll need a flashlight, a bottle of water for each of us, four candy bars, and a small notebook and pen," said Aunt Tabby, ticking things off on her fingers.

"We're not going to stay out all night are we?" asked Pru, wondering why they needed candy bars.

"No, but if one becomes excited their blood sugar sometimes drops too low and a candy bar helps." Aunt Tabby talked with such assurance that neither girl doubted anything she said.

Soon three people with hair hidden under strange bulging dark caps, black jackets and pants, and black tennis shoes walked out the back door. One person had a pack on his/her back and one was jingling car keys. All of them wore dark glasses, but Pru had complained from the time she put them on.

"I can't wear these glasses, especially after dark. I won't be able to see a thing."

"You can see in the dark with these glasses, Pru. I bought them for you girls before I came down here. You're lucky I remembered them, too. They're perfect for this case," said Aunt Tabby.

"I'm always amazed when I buy something that seems to be useless, to find out a few days later, that it is just what is needed for some reason."

They were soon in the car and driving up Vine Street toward the Garden of Eternal Peace. "I hope Miss Cross can find this place." Pru was leaning over the back seat, peering out at the road ahead.

"Unless I've read her wrong, she'll be there." Aunt Tabby pulled to the side of the road in front of the cemetery. A red convertible sport car was parked in front of them.

"I guess that's Miss Cross," said Janie, stepping out of the car. Her foot had just touched the ground when the door on the driver's side of the sport car opened.

A woman with a long dark wig and dark glasses stepped out. She wore a long, dark gray cape that reached the ground. Everybody halted as if they were all in a film that had paused in action. "I am M. K. Cross. Who might you be, sirs?"

Everybody became animated again. "We are the three Musketeers, ready for action," said Janie, trying not to laugh.

"Where can we stash these cars? My car is a real eye catcher." Miss Cross looked around. "Is this a dead end road?"

"No, this road goes on into Henley, but there's an unused road just back there a little ways. It leads to a deserted farm house. You can take the cars back there," said Janie.

Soon the cars were both pulled behind some bushes in a little lay-by on the deserted road. Miss Cross's car was in front and Aunt Tabby's black station wagon was behind it. They got out and walked back to the farmhouse road.

"Unless one was looking for something those cars would never be noticed, but then nobody comes out here anyway. We could have just left them right in the road. I don't think anybody knows about this road." Janie turned to walk back to the main road.

Aunt Tabby looked at Miss Cross. "You drove your car in first. How did you know that lay-by was there?"

Miss Cross grinned. "I've been here a while so I checked this out. I just wanted to see if Janie was a quick as I thought she was, and she is."

Janie turned to look at her. "I didn't think about the lay-by, but I knew it was there. This road hasn't been used in years though."

Soon they had walked back and were through the gate to the Garden of Eternal Peace. Miss Cross looked at Janie. "I think we should go find the grave of William 'Big Boy' Jackson, don't you?"

Pru got a frightened look in her eyes. "Why should we go there? I've thought about it and there's something weird about that tombstone."

"Pru, you didn't think it was weird when we found it. What's wrong with it?" Janie's eyes narrowed speculatively, like Miss Cross's often did.

"Then, I didn't remember that the tall man had said being in the cemetery was better than being 'down there.'"

Aunt Tabby's eyes blared. "That does sound like he

was saying they might be…in deep trouble if they didn't do what somebody told them."

Miss Cross looked at Janie. "It could also mean that he knew more than he was saying, couldn't it Curious Janie Query?"

Janie looked from one face to the other. "I thought about what the tall man said as well, and like Miss Cross, I thought he feared something back over this way. Now, I'm thinking he knows something is down there, but I'm not going to do any guessing until after tonight."

Aunt Tabby shrugged. "Well, come on let's go find 'Big Boy's' grave and then a hiding place and prepare for a long wait."

Evening was closing in as they made their way through the cemetery to the grave. They could still see each other, but soon they wouldn't be able to see anything but bulks or forms. Janie stopped and pointed to the dirt, grass, and leaves that had been clumsily shoved back around the lower part of the tombstone. "The wind didn't blow all this extra stuff up around the stone. Some human hands did this and recently too." Janie stood looking down and started to kick at a tuft of grass, but Miss Cross grabbed her foot.

"Don't disturb anything. That isn't why we're here. We want to see if anyone else is interested in 'Big Boy' Jackson."

Looking around, Janie said, "It's almost totally dark, so let's scatter." They all went looking for places to hide. When Pru switched on her light Aunt Tabby jerked it away from her. "For God's sake, Pru, do you want to be seen?"

Before any of them had settled on one certain place, voices could be heard from the direction of the gate.

A large mausoleum type structure soon hid Aunt Tabby and Pru, who both slid to the ground as close together as they could get. Miss Cross went down the slope and to the left of 'Big Boy's' stone and lowered herself behind a family stone that stretched about five feet across. She looked straight across from where she was and saw Janie's head sink down behind a large statue of Jesus with a lamb on each side of him. Both Janie and Miss Cross were down below the headstone of 'Big Boy's' tomb and were closer to it than Aunt Tabby and Pru. Miss Cross thought this was a good thing since Pru had fainted the first time the men had visited the cemetery.

They still heard voices, but they didn't seem to be moving. Janie edged around the side of one of the lambs and whispered. "Miss Cross, I don't think that's them. They wouldn't stop would they?"

"Shh. I hear footsteps. Listen!" Sure enough muffled and shuffling steps were coming toward where they were hidden.

Soon a faint light was seen and Janie thought *they're near Eliza Marie Hannasett's tomb now.* She crouched lower to the earth and lay very still.

CHAPTER 9

The footsteps came closer and closer. As before, a long crate or box was being carried, but now toward the stone fence boundary instead of away from it. Although two people bore the crate it didn't appear to be really heavy. Their footsteps were quicker and they didn't stop to rest until they reached the tomb of William 'Big Boy' Jackson.

They carried a flashlight with some sort of filter since the light was dim and only illuminated the spot to which it was directed. Now it was directed at the base of the tombstone.

The raspy guttural whisper came through. "Did you leave this mess? Anybody can tell that the wind didn't do this." Pru shifted in her hiding place and Aunt Tabby pulled her closer and turned her head into her own shoulder.

From their hiding places below 'Big Boy's tomb, Miss Cross and Janie stealthily wriggled in their positions in an effort to get a glimpse of the scene. Suddenly the light flashed around and they both dropped behind their cover.

"I heard a noise…like somebody or something," but then a quick breeze came up and the tall man continued with, "I guess it was just the wind. You're right though about the mess I made. I was so glad to be up here I got in a right smart hurry."

"Stop flashing that light around," rasped out a guttural demand. "Let's get this moved," was uttered as the crate was lowered to the ground.

The tall man was slower, but finally lowered his end of the crate as well. "I don't know why your boss, whoever he is, picked the heaviest stone in this cemetery to move."

As Janie and Miss Cross peeped from their hiding places they saw 'Big Boy's' tombstone tilted backwards and laid on the ground. "Whew, that is one heavy rock, but I'd lift ten of them fellers if I didn't have to go down there again," said the tall man.

"Shut up," said the whisperer and picked up his end of the box and took several steps down in the hole where the tombstone had been.

"Now, you're certain that you're coming back out with me, ain't you? I'd die if I had to stay down there by myself. Besides, what if somebody comes along and covers up this hole. I…I jest don't believe I can go down there again."

"I told you I would. We have to stash this first. You come down or it's the big house. Grab your end." The whisperer was gasping between each word, which made him sound more rough and raspy after each gasp. It was difficult to hear or understand him, but the tone let anybody know it was a threat.

When the tall man still hesitated, a small sliver of the moon shone briefly on the metal in the Whisperer's elevated hand. The tall man gasped. "Don't shoot me, I'm comin'. It's jest so hard to do somethin' when I'm tremblin' on the inside like I am." He slowly stooped and picked up his end of the crate and angled it downward into the hole.

The people in hiding lay still and listened as murmured grunts, whispers and curses were heard for a few minutes and then all was quiet. Aunt Tabby peeped around the edge of her hiding place. "Are they gone?"

Miss Cross crawled around the edge of the family stone, but didn't stand up. "We can't hear them anymore, but they may be able to hear us," she whispered.

Janie stood up and walked to the hole left open and bending down briefly flashed her light inside. She quickly turned off her light again and whispered. "I can't see them. There are steps. This must be a secret tunnel or something."

Miss Cross stood up. "I'm going to follow them," she whispered. She changed her mind though when a car screeched to a halt near the gate.

Everyone quickly found their hiding places again and just in time, too. Two voices were heard as well as hurrying footsteps.

"I don't like graveyards, especially at night, but a hundred dollars apiece is a lot of money to just cover up the hole made when a tombstone fell over."

The person attached to the voice wasn't close enough to make out whether he was tall, short, old or young. Both seemed to be in a hurry to earn their money since they were almost running when they came into view. Their flashlights cast a wide beam, but the light was shining in front of them and they still couldn't be fully seen.

"That whisperin' man said he'd get us out of that jail sentence we're certain to get, and give us a hundred besides if we'd come out here at nine-thirty tonight and put that tombstone back in place," said another voice really close to where Pru and Aunt Tabby were hid.

Janie and Miss Cross heard a sound cut off suddenly and froze in place.

"What was that? Did you hear something?" The voice was shaky.

"Aw Joe, you're the scariest feller I ever seen. Who would come into a graveyard on a night this dark? Well, we did, but we're getting' paid," said his partner, softly chuckling.

"Well, I heard something." Joe stood silently listening.

"You probably heard your own heart about to jump out. Fear will do that to you," said the other voice.

Sounding calmer now, Joe said, "Dale, how you reckon that whisperin' feller found out about a hole being in the cemetery?"

"Well, duh! It was probably his kinfolk's grave or else he wouldn't pay us to close it up, would he?" The voices passed the hiding place of Pru and Aunt Tabby with their flashlights casting beams of light to the right and left. Finally they neared the opened grave or whatever it was.

"Here it is Joe. Well, I want you to looky here. I've

been in this graveyard a hundred times, I guess, and I ain't never seen nothing like this, have you?" Dale stood shining his light down the hole that had been covered by 'Big Boy' Jackson's tombstone. Joe walked up beside him.

"God Almighty! This ain't no grave a' tall. I wonder where them steps go to." Joe stooped down and circled his light first to one side and then to the other side.

"This is some kind of tunnel and it wouldn't put there for show. This may lead to a secret stash of some kind. I wonder what they're hiding, don't you?" Joe turned to look at his buddy who wasn't holding his shovels very steady.

"No. I'm not gettin' paid to wonder, so let's hurry and put that tombstone back in place and get out of here. This place is giving me the willies."

Dale had been the brave one, but seeing the tunnel and the steps made him think of the dark steps his drunken father had kicked him down too many times in the past. He quickly walked to the head of the tombstone and stood waiting. He had dropped the shovels he'd been carrying on the other side of the hole.

"Come on, Joe. It'll take both of us to lift this thing and we ain't got all night. We're supposed to be through and out of this cemetery in an hour and a half. We've wasted a lot of time already."

Joe walked down the side of the hole and soon both men were straining and cursing. When the tombstone was finally lifted and shoved back in place both men heaved a sigh of relief. "A man could bust a gut liftin' that kind of load and then the doctor would charge more than a hundred dollars to treat it. I think we got cheated, Dale."

Dale started shoveling the dirt, leaves, and grass up around the bottom of the tombstone and Joe stooped to help. They were almost finished when a hoot owl flew into a nearby tree and gave a loud hoot. Shovels went flying and so did the men as they ran from the cemetery cursing all the way.

The four witnesses remained in hiding for another five minutes until they heard the car start and then cautiously crept out.

"Turn on your light, Janie. I want to see if everyone is all right." Aunt Tabby reached down to help Pru, but couldn't find her. She had no light and was frantically fumbling around without feeling a body.

"Pru's not here. Pru, where are you? Get over here with that flashlight, Janie. Something has happened to Pru."

Both Miss Cross and Janie hurried to where Aunt Tabby and Pru had been hiding. Janie pointed the light toward Aunt Tabby and then down to the ground and saw a crumpled heap a foot away to the right.

"There's Pru. She's fainted again." Janie fell to her knees beside of Pru and grasped her shoulders. "Pru, Pru, wake up. They're all gone. Wake up!"

"Here, let me see what I can do?" Miss Cross opened Janie's back pack and took out a bottle of water. She took off the top and poured water into her hand and dashed it into Pru's face.

Pru's eyes opened wide and she sat up sputtering. "Who poured water on me? I'm all wet." Suddenly remembering where she was, she started shivering.

Aunt Tabby took over. "Pru, honey, it's all over.

There's nobody here but us. We're safe and as soon as you can walk we can go back to our cars and go home."

That speech had the desired effect. Pru struggled to her feet with Janie and Aunt Tabby helping her and together they made their way out of the Garden of Eternal Peace. In the road they stopped. Miss Cross wasn't with them.

"Stay here, I'll go check on Miss Cross," said Janie just as Miss Cross appeared.

She had taken off her cape and was carrying something all wrapped up in it.

"What is that?" asked Aunt Tabby.

"The shovels, they'll have fingerprints on them." She and Janie were not really close to Pru and Aunt Tabby, but she leaned nearer to Janie and whispered.

"Janie, those boys left those poor men down in that hole unless someone gets them out or there's an opening at the other end." Miss Cross put her bundle into Janie's arms and fished her keys from her pocket.

"Well, darn. Our cars aren't here, but we need to keep those shovels. I'll have to carry them to the car, I guess."

Janie gasped. "That's right. That tall man was afraid the Whisperer wouldn't come back out with him, and I don't believe he will, do you?"

"No, I don't. I think the Whisperer needed some help and he conned that tall man into helping him. I'll bet if anybody is left down there it'll be the tall man," whispered Miss Cross as she dusted her hands off on her pants.

"Janie you'd better stay here with Pru while Aunt Tabby and I get the cars. " She looked at Pru who had begun to tremble again.

"Don't leave us here! I can walk." Pru was shaking now, so Aunt Tabby and Janie put Pru between them leaving Miss Cross to follow with her burden of shovels. They all walked down the road to get the cars.

When they reached the farmhouse road, Miss Cross suddenly stopped. "Janie let me borrow that light, please." Janie passed it to her and she pointed its beam on the roadway. Definite tire tracks showed clearly on the farmhouse road. Miss Cross looked at Janie.

"What do you think of this?" Janie followed the tracks a few feet and stopped.

"These are probably the tracks you and Aunt Tabby made coming out here."

Miss Cross let out a long sigh. "Shoot, I thought I'd found another clue in this case."

"I think we'd better hurry. Those men that went down in that hole will be in a panic when they come back and find there's no way out," said Janie.

"Oh Heavens, that's right. Those poor, poor men," said Aunt Tabby.

Miss Cross went a step or two in front of the others and when they got to the lay-by she stopped. "Bring the light here, Curious Janie. Look at this. It is just what I suspected. They're using that old farmhouse, I'll bet."

Janie put the beam of her light on the roadway and it was plain that a car or some vehicle had recently traveled on that road. She turned to Miss Cross. "Let's go out to the farmhouse and take a look."

"Oh no, you're not, Janie. Your mother would have me arrested. If they have anything out there, they'll also have a guard. We've been in enough danger tonight." Aunt Tabby had a definite sound to her voice.

"She's right, Curious Janie. We don't want to run into guard dogs or a gun and besides Pru isn't feeling well and needs to go home," said Miss Cross.

Janie relented and stood holding onto Pru while Miss Cross directed Aunt Tabby as she backed out of the lay-by. Janie opened Aunt Tabby's door and helped Pru inside. Miss Cross took a little longer since she had to stow the shovels, but she backed out without help and just in time too. As soon as Miss Cross's car was in the roadway, Janie opened her car door to ask what their next step would be when two bright green eyes appeared and a ferocious growl erupted. Janie jumped into Miss Cross's car and slammed the door. Aunt Tabby pulled out and Miss Cross was right behind her with the dog barking and snarling beside them as they went.

CHAPTER 10

When they pulled onto the main road the dog gave up and both cars sped away. The girls discarded their disguises as they rode along, but the cars stopped a little farther down the road. There Aunt Tabby and Miss Cross shed their disguises too. Pru was still not feeling well, so they drove to Pru's house first.

When they pulled into the Leery driveway, Miss Cross and Janie got out of Miss Cross's car and came up to the window of Aunt Tabby's car. "Pru, are you going to tell your mother what happened?" Miss Cross asked.

"I don't know what to tell her, and I don't want to lie," said Pru.

"You could say we were walking by the cemetery and some men were there and you got scared," said Janie. She looked at Miss Cross. "That wouldn't be a lie, would it?"

"That hoot owl scared the pants off those young

fellers, so that could be another reason Pru got scared," said Aunt Tabby.

"Yes, and when they started running Pru was afraid they were after us," said Miss Cross. She smiled and looked around. "Well, if Pru hadn't fainted she would have thought that, since they were running towards where she and Aunt Tabby were hidden."

Just then Mrs. Leery came to the door. "Pru, is that you?"

"It's us, Aunt Audrey. We were just talking. Pru got scared and she's not feeling too good right now."

"You've been gone three hours. I want all of you to come in. I don't want any of Janie's wild tales, I want a grown-up version," said Mrs. Leery.

"Aunt Audrey, it took longer because Aunt Tabby doesn't walk fast anymore." Janie gave Mrs. Leery an angry stare before winking at Aunt Tabby, who rolled her eyes in a 'Don't use me' look.

"I'm not talking about how fast you walked, Janie, but we all know where your curiosity can lead the both of you. Come on in and I'll make some hot cocoa."

The four weary adventurers trooped into the Leery living room and took seats around the room.

Mr. Leery, who was seated in front of the television, raised the remote in his hand to eye level and clicked off the television. He was a very quiet and somewhat introverted man so his action startled both Janie and Pru. They looked at each other with a 'oops! We're in for it now' glance.

Nobody said a word until Mrs. Leery came into

the room bearing a tray with six cups. She passed cocoa around and then placed the tray on the floor, beside her chair, before taking a seat facing Miss Cross.

"Well, for starters, Miss Cross, I want you to know that this is not the first time that Pru has returned sick after a trip with Janie. Also, I've known Tabby Martin since we were children and she was a young Curious Janie Query. So, you will understand why I would like to hear your version of this three-hour hike."

For a moment, Miss Cross sat up a little taller in her seat and got that narrowed-eye look that Janie always noticed.

"Well, as you know, Janie and Pru are students in my seventh grade science class and I like both of them. Until the carnival I had never met or talked to them outside of the classroom, though. I didn't even know they would be at the carnival, but as they were going to buy tickets for the Roller Coaster, Janie saw me and stopped to introduce her Aunt Tabby. I was talking to a man from the bank and Janie thought she recognized his voice. She thought she'd heard his voice before and since you know Janie, you will understand her curiosity."

Miss Cross stopped and sat thinking. "I could tell Janie wanted to ask me something, but was wary about it. Finally, she asked me who the man was and I told her. Then we all started talking and Janie told me that she, Pru, and her Aunt Tabby were going on a hike one evening and asked if I wanted to go with them. Since I don't know many people in this area and sometimes get bored, I took them up on their invitation."

Everybody sat still as if absorbing this speech, until Mr. Leery said, "That's not an explanation of why Pru got scared or where you were when she got scared."

This was so unusual for Mr. Leery that even his wife's eyes widened. Miss Cross's eyes narrowed to slits. "Pru was frightened when an owl hooted and these two men came running toward her. She fainted, I think, because the men were running out of the cemetery."

"Where were all of you when this happened?" Mrs. Leery jumped in on the inquisition.

Aunt Tabby took up the explanation. "We parked our cars near the cemetery and began our walk from there because that road doesn't have a lot of traffic."

"Did this happen when you first parked or later?" Mr. Leery seemed really interested.

"Later Uncle Henry, we left as soon as we got in the cars, after Pru got so scared." Janie looked around at her audience. "It was dark and everything was so quiet and then that owl hooted. That's when we heard the running footsteps. It was enough to scare anybody."

That seemed to satisfy Mr. Leery since he picked up his remote and the television blared on again.

It must have satisfied Mrs. Leery as well. She picked up the tray from the floor and started out of the room. She turned. "Well, I'm glad all of you are home, but Pru can't go on any more hikes if they're going to be three hours long."

Janie, Miss Cross, and Aunt Tabby rose from their seats. "Thanks, Mrs. Leery for the cocoa. It hit the spot," said Miss Cross and turned to the door.

"Good night, Audrey and Henry," said Aunt Tabby and was echoed by Janie as they went out the door.

When they were back at the cars they all stopped. "I'm going to report what we discovered tonight to that person I was telling you about. This person will take care of it and never bring any of our names into it," said Miss Cross in a low voice.

Aunt Tabby was standing with her arm around Janie's shoulders. "Yes, I think that's best. Make sure they know that those poor men are probably hysterical down in the tunnel if they haven't had heart attacks and died. You'll let us know, won't you?"

"I sure will." She turned to Janie. "Miss Curious Janie Query, I think your curiosity has hit pay dirt tonight."

Janie put out her hand to have it clasped by Miss Cross. "Thanks Miss Cross. I'm glad we met."

Miss Cross smiled. "Thank you, Curious Janie Query, and don't you ever stop being curious, but don't you dare take any more dangerous risks either."

Aunt Tabby put out her hand and shook Miss Cross's hand. "It's been fun. It's too bad we didn't meet when I was a wee bit younger."

Miss Cross punched her lightly on the shoulder. "Don't you try to pull that 'too old' thing on me. I know that look you had on your face. If Janie hadn't been with us, you would have gone right down that tunnel with me, wouldn't you?"

Aunt Tabby grinned and opened her car door. "I might have at that."

Soon both drivers pulled out and were on their

separate paths to their quiet homes and beds, or so they thought.

Before they pulled out of the driveway, Mr. Leery had gone to his study and picked up the phone.

Miss Cross drove on past the town of Willowdale to a pay telephone booth. She had an extended conversation before she hung up. Looking carefully around, she left the booth, and taking a round-about route returned to her apartment.

The next day several people reported being awakened by police sirens and one old man said, "They must have been arrestin' dead people, for the cemetery was full of lights and noise."

When Janie went down to breakfast the next morning the television was blaring. "Charlie Dennis was the man found in the tunnel. He's in the hospital with an apparent heart attack." Janie nodded her head knowingly and thought, *Miss Cross and I had it right. The Whisperer did plan to leave him down there.*

The news continued with "The police got an anonymous tip about ten o'clock last night and when they went to investigate they found a tunnel leading from the cemetery to a bank vault. Charlie Dennis was found in the tunnel. He was unresponsive, but is now in intensive care at the local hospital. Several thousand pounds of cocaine were found and three people have already been arrested. Authorities suspect that one of the three is the other man reported to have gone down in the tunnel with Dennis. It is believed that he exited through the bank vault door, and left Dennis in the tunnel.

Aunt Tabby came into the kitchen yawning and rubbing her eyes, but hearing the tail end of the news, she stopped in startled amazement. Janie jumped up and ran to her. She gave her a hug and whispered, "Don't say anything."

"What's happened?" she said, hugging Janie in return.

"There were some big doings in the cemetery last night, Tabby. You all hiked the wrong way and missed all the excitement," said Mr. Query.

"What was it? Did they find people robbing graves or something?"

"No, it was bigger than that. They busted a cocaine drug ring that certain people have been working on for about a year. Until someone called in an anonymous tip last night, the Narcotics Bureau hadn't been able to find out how it was being slipped into this area."

"A drug ring!" Janie's eyes were as round as saucers. "Did you hear that, Aunt Tabby? A drug ring with big time crooks. I just can't believe it."

Jimmy laughed. "Yeah, ain't it a shame, Janie. With all your sleuthing you still didn't get to solve a big case like that."

Aunt Tabby looked at Janie and smiled. "I'll bet Janie could have solved it if she was a little older."

"Tabitha Martin, don't you encourage her. She keeps me worried to death with her sleuthing already." Mary Ann Query looked across at Janie and smiled. "I love her though."

"I wonder who tipped off the cops, but I guess we'll never know. The police protect their informers, or so I've been told," said Jimmy, looking wise.

"Janie, you'd better hurry and eat your breakfast. You'll be late for school," cautioned Mrs. Query.

Janie wolfed down her cereal and jumped to her feet. "I can't wait to tell Pru. She'll not believe her ears...a drug bust, right here in Willowdale."

Pru was jumping from one foot to the other when Janie appeared. "Janie, did you hear the news this morning?" She lowered her voice. "We actually helped solve a major crime, didn't we?"

Janie grabbed her arm. "Pru, promise me that you won't even hint that we know anything about that. We could be in danger."

Pru jerked her arm away. "I'm not stupid, Janie. Daddy was up really early this morning and he made me promise that I'd not say anything about being anywhere near the Garden of Eternal Peace last night."

Janie's eyes lit up. "Why was Uncle Henry up early? I thought he was on the night shift."

"He is, but he came in just as I went down for breakfast. He looked like he hadn't been asleep." Pru stood thinking. "He still had his work clothes on. That's strange, isn't it?"

Janie suddenly remembered his strange behavior last night and her eyes narrowed. "Yes, Pru, that is very strange, but we'll be late, so let's run.

CHAPTER 11

Their first class was English and they had already been marked tardy. "Both of you go to the office and have your names taken off the absence list." The teacher gave them a stern look and they hurried out the door.

The whole school could talk of nothing but the drug bust. "If the informer is ever caught he'll be lucky if he lives," said Kyle Jester when they were eating lunch.

"Did they catch the boss or the kingpin or whatever those people are called?" asked Janie.

Kyle shook his head. "I don't know, but I'll bet Dad knows. If he doesn't know, it will still be all over the news this evening."

When they went to science class Miss Cross was busy writing on the blackboard. She turned as they all took their seats. "How many of you remembered to study

Chapter 12? I hope all of you did, because I have a pop quiz ready for you."

Moans and sighs were heard around the room as well as desks shifting as several students began looking in their desks.

"It's too late to look for your notes now. Get out a single sheet of paper and your pen or pencil. Clear your desk of everything else. Put your name on the top right-hand corner, the date on the top left-hand corner, and then number your paper to twenty down the left-hand side." Miss Cross stood tapping her pencil against her chin in a thoughtful manner.

Janie tried to catch Miss Cross's eye, in hopes of getting a nod or something, but Miss Cross completely ignored her. Janie followed all of the instructions given and then looked across at Pru and raised her eyebrows. Pru shrugged her shoulders. Janie didn't know how much Pru had studied, but she knew she had only read the notes twice and hadn't really studied at all.

Miss Cross turned from the blackboard. "These words are the answers to the questions, but they are not in the correct order. You will have had to study to get all twenty correct. Listen carefully. I'll read each question slowly and will read it once more upon request, but only one more time. Ready?"

For the rest of the class period students were listening, writing, and groaning. When the last question was read many sighs were heard, but there were no vocal protests. They knew by the clock that it was time for the bell and began putting their things together.

Janie and Pru were very slow and methodical as they organized their backpacks and straightened their desks. The bell rang, but they were not finished. They kept at it until everyone had left the room except themselves and Miss Cross.

"Miss Cross," began Janie, but stopped when Miss Cross put her finger on her lips in a signal for silence. She looked at Janie and shook her head.

"Yes, Miss Query. Do you have a question?"

"I don't think I did well on this test. The police and sirens went by our house all night and I couldn't study," said Janie, giving Miss Cross an intent look.

"I'm sure you're not the only one, Miss Query. You should have studied on Friday night or Saturday. Right now, I think you girls need to get a move on. I have these papers to score. Goodbye girls, I'll see you tomorrow."

Janie and Pru slung their backpacks on and started out of the room just as Mr. Walker, the principal opened the door. Janie eased past him and said, as she went out the door, "I tried to study, Pru. I don't think she's being very fair, do you?"

They both went stalking angrily down the hall to the exit and jerked the door open. Once outside they looked around to see if anyone was watching them. A few other students were standing in groups talking while waiting for their buses, but they saw none of the teachers or custodians.

Janie whispered, "Keep acting mad, Pru. There could be people looking out the windows."

They tried to walk as if they were angry or at least

upset all the way to the traffic light. Once they had crossed the street they relaxed and stopped.

"Janie, why do you suppose Miss Cross motioned for us to not say anything?"

Janie walked a few steps. "I don't know, Pru, unless she thinks her room is bugged or something. I thought it was strange that the Principal came just as we were leaving, didn't you?"

"Yes it was. Mr. Walker never comes to rooms. He calls people on the intercom if he wants something."

Janie shrugged and kept walking. "Maybe Miss Cross will get word to us in some way, but she may not if she is suspected. I don't know why she would be suspected though, unless we have been watched."

"Why would anybody be watching us? We're not spies. Oh, I guess the word is out about you being so curious about everything," said Pru, looking worried.

"Pru, I don't think anybody is watching us. The police would have been to our house already if that was the case." They had reached the intersection and parted, both still thoughtful.

When Janie went through her front door Aunt Tabby was waiting for her.

"Janie, your mom and dad have gone to the hospital to see Charlie Dennis, the man left in the tunnel. He was the gardener for your grandmother Query before she died and your daddy knows him."

"Is he better? I thought he was in intensive care."

"He is and they may not even get to see him. If it hadn't been dark I might have recognized him the other night, but I wouldn't have gotten to see him anyway. Pru almost gave us away. If I hadn't jerked her face into my shoulder they would have certainly heard her cry out. She fainted, of course, and after that I was safe, but couldn't move since she was laying half on top of me." Aunt Tabby still seemed agitated.

"You're acting all keyed up, Aunt Tabby. What's wrong?"

"Janie, the police may come to question you and Pru."

Janie's eyes widened. "Police…question me. Why?"

"I don't know that they will, but Pru's mother called and said since we were out walking that night, we may all be questioned. Aunt Tabby turned toward the kitchen.

"Come on in the kitchen, so I can crochet and talk. I'm making an afghan."

Janie dropped her backpack behind the door and followed Aunt Tabby to take a seat at the kitchen table. "I sure hope they don't question Pru. She'll get scared and blurt out the whole thing."

Aunt Tabby pulled out a chair across from Janie and sat down with a sigh. "Well, if they do, they do. You girls did nothing wrong. Actually none of us did anything wrong. We just witnessed something that could anger some people who are dangerous."

Aunt Tabby shook her head. "It's hard to believe that my hometown, the most peaceful place on God's green Earth, has been sheltering a drug ring."

"Do Dad and Mom know about this, I mean about us being questioned?"

"I don't think so, because Audrey called just before

you came home. Of course, she could have called Mary Ann's cell phone."

Janie sat at the table deep in thought. "Aunt Tabby, I'm scared. This all started when I decided to check out Kyle Jester's tales about things being missing in town and then Henry Mercer saying that lights had been seen in the cemetery. I really thought Kyle was telling tall tales and I was just going to prove him wrong."

Aunt Tabby was also thinking. "Janie, do you remember all of us going to the cemetery at least once each month and putting flowers on your grandparents' grave?"

"Yeah, we'd always go to Grandpa's tree, you know where his initials are carved. Daddy would always lift me high enough to see Grandpa's initials carved in the tree. Why do you ask?"

"I just thought that if you should be asked why you were in the cemetery you could say you were going to your Grandpa's grave, couldn't you?" asked Aunt Tabby.

Janie brightened up. "Yeah, that's a good idea and I did show Pru how much the tree had grown by how high up on it the initials were."

A car pulled into the driveway and they both jumped to their feet. Aunt Tabby put her arm around Janie who had moved to her side. They stood waiting for the doorbell, but it didn't ring. The door opened instead.

Janie ran to her dad and put her arms around his waist. "We thought you were the police," said Janie, hugging her dad.

"That's why we hurried back. Your Aunt Audrey

called us and we thought you'd want us here, should that happen," said Mr. Query, hugging her close.

"I don't think they'll even question you girls. You were just in the road in front of the cemetery...but they could want to know if you'd seen anything. You did see those two men running, though."

Mrs. Query shook her head. "Well, they might want to talk to you, but you haven't done anything wrong, so it won't amount to much."

"Not unless the drug dealers think we reported them. I'd rather have the police questioning me as to have drug dealers suspicious," said Janie, still standing in the protection of her father's arms.

Mrs. Query had brought some bags in with her, which were now on the table. She began taking food from the bags. "We stopped by Captain D's on the way home and brought fish dinners for each of us. I hope nobody hungry drops in before we get to eat."

Mr. Query looked down at Janie. "I don't think you have anything to worry about, but should the police want to question you, your mother and I are here for you, Curious Janie. Try not to worry."

They had finished their meal and gone to the living room to watch the news when the doorbell rang. Mr. Query went to answer it. He came back with Pru and her parents.

Pru was pale and looked so upset that Janie went to her and put her arm around her. "Pru, what's wrong?" All the adults had moved on into the kitchen and taken seats around the table. Pru and Janie followed them before Pru answered.

"Daddy says the police are apt to question us. He thinks we should make sure we have the same story." A puzzled look passed between Pru and Janie.

"Uncle Henry, has anyone said anything to you about us? I mean how would anyone know anything at all about us unless somebody in the family mentioned us?"

Henry Leery shook his head. "Who would I talk to? I'm not on the police force. I just thought that someone may have seen you four walking the night this happened and reported it."

Pru spoke up. "It was dark and they wouldn't have known us anyway."

Aunt Tabby was sitting beside Pru and quickly nudged her leg under the table. "It was dark before we saw anyone, wasn't it?" Aunt Tabby had taken over to hinder Pru from mentioning that they had worn disguises.

Pru suddenly realized what Aunt Tabby had prevented. She was now red instead of pale white. "Yes, it was really dark. I couldn't see those running men at all, but I sure did hear them."

They all sat talking about the investigation, but stopped when the phone rang. Janie jumped to her feet to answer it. "Yes, this is she. No, not yet. They are? We didn't give that. No, those were made-up." Janie chuckled. "I sure hope so. Good-bye." When she turned from the phone every eye was trained on her.

"Well, who was that, Janie?" asked Mrs. Query. "Whoever it was certainly asked a lot of questions."

"That was Miss Cross. She was thinking the same thing that Uncle Henry is worried about. She wanted to know if the police had been here. I told her no...You all heard that."

Henry Leery scooted back in his chair. "What else did she say, Janie? Why did you say, 'we didn't give that' and 'no, those were made up'?"

Janie hesitated for a moment. She was unsure of how to explain it without giving too much away. She tried an evasive tactic.

"Uncle Henry you sound just like a detective. Are you sure you don't have a second job?" Janie was stunned at the fleeting expression on his face, but everyone else laughed.

"Janie, stop trying to evade the question," said Mr. Query chuckling at the idea of the reticent, self-effacing Henry Leery being accused of being a detective.

"I'm not being evasive, Dad. I was just shocked that something as innocent as Pru and I talking to three strangers one evening would get involved in this. Do you remember when I told you about meeting two women and a man when Pru and I were playing? Well, they must have told the police that they met us, but for the life of me I don't know why." Janie looked at Uncle Henry to see his reaction.

"Maybe it was because they were interested in the cemetery. You didn't give them your names did you?" asked Mr. Query.

"No, and the names we did mention were made-up," said Pru as she remembered Arbutus Matilda Macintosh.

"Well, unless the police want to look all over town for two girls about your size, that won't amount to much, will it?" Mrs. Query looked around for confirmation.

CHAPTER 12

Except for the daily papers and the nightly news nothing was said in either household about the case until Friday of the following week. When the girls arrived at school that morning there was a hushed atmosphere. As they went down the hall to first period class, Kyle Jester motioned Janie and Pru toward his locker where he was getting books. "Mr. Walker has been arrested," he whispered.

"Mr. Walker!" gasped Pru.

"Why was he arrested?" whispered Janie. Kyle whispered back that he was involved in the drug ring.

"How do you know? I'll bet it's just a wild rumor," said Janie.

"No, Dad heard it on the police scanner. Dad said that a lot of heads will roll before this case is finished." Finally Kyle fished his needed book out of the locker just as the bell rang.

The three quickly went to their classes. In the first class the atmosphere was subdued and other teachers frequently came in and whispered something to the teacher and then left. It was the same in the other classes. The students knew that something had happened, but didn't know what it was.

In science class, Kyle Jester asked, "Miss Cross, why are all the halls so quiet? It's almost like there are no students here today and all the teachers are whispering among themselves?"

Miss Cross hesitated. "I've heard some rumors, Kyle, but I won't say anything until it is verified in the news. I guess you people will listen to the news this evening, won't you?"

"Mr. Walker must be sick. He's not been on the intercom all day." Janie hoped to get a reaction from Miss Cross and she did.

"I believe he is very sick today. That intercom breaks the monotony of the day, doesn't it?" Miss Cross smiled and looked at Janie.

Janie couldn't wait to get home and when the bell rang she and Pru were the first ones out the door. They ran to the light at the intersection and were soon nearing Ivy Road.

"Janie, do you think Miss Cross knew that Mr. Walker had been arrested? I thought she was trying to tell us something when she said she believed he was very sick today."

"She was letting us know that the rumor was true. I wish I could talk to her, but I'm afraid to, right now."

"I thought she stressed that we should watch the news," said Pru as they came to the Ivy Road cutoff.

Janie stopped dead in her tracks. "She did, didn't she? Thanks Pru for bringing that to my attention. Let's hurry home. I don't want to miss anything."

Janie made it home faster than she ever had before. As she opened the door she said, "Mom, have you been listening to the news?" Mrs. Query wasn't in the living room and Janie hurried to the kitchen. She wasn't there, either, but Aunt Tabby came in from the kitchen patio.

"Where's Mom?"

"Your Aunt Audrey came by and they went to some orchard. Their apples are on sale. Did you need her?"

Janie sank dejectedly into a chair by the table. "Aunt Tabby, I was so sure that the news would have more about the drug bust today. I heard at school that our principal, Mr. Walker, was arrested. Have you heard anything?"

"No, but I haven't had the television or radio on. Mary Ann wanted me to bake my old time apple stack cake and it takes all day."

"Shucks!" Janie rose and went to the refrigerator for some tea and came back to her chair just as Jimmy came in from college.

"Well, heads are rolling today. Have you heard the news?" Jimmy asked as he too went for the tea.

"Turn the television on, Jimmy, and we'll all go to the living room," said Aunt Tabby, rinsing her hands in the sink.

They settled into seats facing the television when the news came on.

"Willowdale is rife with accusations, charges, and innuendoes and there have been several arrests. A huge stash of cocaine, marijuana, and prescription drugs were found in an empty safe vault at Settlers Bank and Trust. The President, Jon Millinger, has been arrested along with his loan officer, Clive Scaler. The dispatcher, who turned out to be Robert Walker, our school principal, has also been arrested as well as the man found in the tunnel beneath the Garden of Eternal Peace." The news reporter went on to say that an abandoned farmhouse had been the living quarters for the dealers when they brought a load in and took the pay out.

Janie sat listening attentively since she had only been involved for the past few weeks. She looked at Aunt Tabby and smiled. Aunt Tabby smiled and winked knowingly.

The reporter then switched to a news briefing by Gordon Beecher, Police Chief of Willowdale, who recapped what they had just heard. Then the briefing was opened for questions and the first questioner asked, "Who or how did you break this case? I know you said the drug ring had been operating for three years, but you haven't said what happened or who tipped you off about this drug ring."

The police chief smiled. "This is hard to believe, but like the 'straw that broke the camel's back,' a little girl recognized the voice of Clive Scaler."

Upon further questioning by various reporters it was revealed that, although the little girl never saw his face, she did recognize the voice and mentioned it where an undercover agent could hear it.

Another reporter asked if they knew who the little girl was and the Police Chief said no, that they hadn't been able to locate her, but that another agent reported that two little girls had been in our local cemetery looking for the grave of a relative by the name of McIntosh. This agent thought it was strange, because usually little girls do not like cemeteries.

"Did anyone find that grave?"

The police chief shook his head. "No, if there was such a person they're not buried in our cemetery."

Janie sat listening and wondering who was the agent, the man, or one of the two women she and Pru had met. Also she knew that she hadn't said anything about Clive Scaler to anyone except Aunt Tabby and Miss Cross. Now she looked at Aunt Tabby with a narrowed gaze.

Mrs. Query came back just then. "Jimmy, will you go bring in the apples from my car? I put them in two boxes so they wouldn't be too heavy to carry.

"Mom, where's Dad? He's never this late," said Janie.

"He called me on his cell phone. They're having a special city council meeting tonight. They've caught most of the people involved in that drug ring, I think,"

"Why would the city council have to meet? I thought that was police work," said Aunt Tabby.

"It is police work, but the president of the bank was arrested and so was the school principal. I suppose they'll have to decide what they need to do in both cases."

"The bank is owned by the stockholders, isn't it? If so, then the board would have to make that decision, wouldn't it?" asked Jimmy who was studying business management in college.

"Will they shut the school down?" Janie didn't want that to happen.

"No, the school board can hire another man to take over, but the vice-principal can serve until they find one." Jimmy had just done a project involving a similar matter and now had an opportunity to show off his knowledge.

A car pulled into the driveway and Mr. Query got out. Mrs. Query turned to Aunt Tabby. "Did you get that cake made?"

"Yes and the casserole is in the oven. I still need to bake the rolls, but that only takes ten minutes."

"Good. I know John will be hungry. To tell the truth I'm hungry too and those delicious smells coming from the kitchen are not one bit of help." Mrs. Query laughed and turned to Janie.

"Go wash your hands and set the table for dinner. I don't want to make your daddy wait much longer."

Janie started toward the kitchen, but turned back quickly when she heard another reporter speak up. "Did the little girl know Mr. Scaler's name?

"No, but she certainly give him a very fitting name," said the police chief with a wide grin.

"What name did she give him?" asked the reporter with a rapt expression.

The police chief laughed merrily. "She called him "The Whisperer."

www.ingramcontent.com/pod-product-compliance
Ingram Content Group UK Ltd.
Pitfield, Milton Keynes, MK11 3LW, UK
UKHW040019200726
13854UKWH00001B/266